cult ficti...

Cult Fiction is a free sampler containing ten excerpts from cutting-edge novelists. Mixing the classic with the new, *Cult Fiction* takes you on a white-knuckle ride through some of the darkest and most extreme visions in modern literature: urban nightmares, men and women on the edge, and societies about to implode. Essential reading for those who like their fiction hardboiled, hungry and a little bit trippy.

cocaine nights – j g ballard

naked lunch – william burroughs

microserfs – douglas coupland

bordersnakes – james crumley

florida roadkill – tim dorsey

the restraint of beasts – magnus mills

253 – geoff ryman

one of us – michael marshall smith

murder book – richard rayner

let's put the future behind us – jack womack

Cult Fiction also contains ten £1-off vouchers –
see back pages for details.

cult fiction

Flamingo

An Imprint of HarperCollins*Publishers*

Flamingo
An Imprint of HarperCollins*Publishers*
77–85 Fulham Palace Road,
Hammersmith, London W6 8JB

www.**fire**and**water**.com

This collection first published by Flamingo 1999

Individual copyrights:
Cocaine Nights © J.G. Ballard 1996
Naked Lunch © William Burroughs 1959, 1964, 1982, 1991
Microserfs © Douglas Coupland 1995
Bordersnakes © James Crumley 1996
Florida Roadkill © Tim Dorsey 1999
The Restraint of Beasts © Magnus Mills 1998
253 © Geoff Ryman 1996, 1998
One of Us © Michael Marshall Smith 1998
Murder Book © Richard Rayner 1997
Let's Put the Future Behind Us © Jack Womack 1996

ISBN 0 00 651407 3

Typeset in Linotype Bembo by
Rowland Phototypesetting Ltd, Bury St Edmunds, Suffolk

Printed and bound in Great Britain by
Clays Ltd, St Ives plc

CONTENTS

J.G. Ballard

Cocaine Nights

'**Utterly compulsive. One is constantly being brought up short by the sheer strangeness of Ballard's imagination.**'
Sunday Telegraph

Five people die in an unexplained housefire in the Spanish resort of Estrella de Mar, an exclusive enclave for the rich, retired British, centred around the thriving Club Nautico. The manager of the club, Frank Prentice, pleads guilty to charges of murder – yet not even the police believe him. When his brother Charles arrives to unravel the truth, he gradually discovers that behind the resort's civilised facade there is a secret world of crime, drugs and illicit sex . . .

At once an engrossing mystery and an unnerving vision of a society coming to terms with unlimited leisure, *Cocaine Nights* is a stunningly original work of the imagination from one of Britain's leading writers – at the forefront of modern fiction writing for over three decades.

―――――――――

J.G. Ballard was born in 1930 in Shanghai, China. After the attack on Pearl Harbor, he and his family were placed in a civilian prison camp. They returned to England in 1946. After working on a scientific journal, he published his first novel, *The Drowned World*, in 1961. Subsequent novels include *The Drought, The Crystal World, Crash, High-Rise* and *Empire of the Sun*, which won the *Guardian* Fiction Prize and was shortlisted for the Booker Prize. It was later filmed by Steven Spielberg. His most recent novels are *The Kindness of Women* and *Rushing to Paradise*. *Cocaine Nights*, a *Sunday Times* bestseller in hardback and paperback, was shortlisted for the 1996 Whitbread Novel Award.

Cocaine Nights
Available now from Flamingo
ISBN 0 00 655064 9

An Incident in the Car Park

ESTRELLA DE MAR was coming out to play. From the balcony of Frank's apartment, three floors above the swimming pool, I watched the members of the Club Nautico take their places in the sun. Tennis players swung their rackets as they set off for the courts, warming up for three hard-fought sets. Sunbathers loosened the tops of their swimsuits and oiled themselves beside the pool, pressing their lip-gloss to the icy, salty rims of the day's first margaritas. An open-cast gold mine of jewellery lay among the burnished breasts. The hubbub of gossip seemed to dent the surface of the pool, and indiscretion ruled as the members happily debriefed each other on the silky misdemeanours of the night.

To David Hennessy, who hovered behind me among the clutter of Frank's possessions, I commented: 'What handsome women . . . the *jeunesse dorée* of the Club Nautico. Here that means anyone under sixty.'

'Absolutely, dear chap. Come to Estrella de Mar and throw away the calendar.' He joined me at the rail, sighing audibly. 'Aren't they a magnificent sight? Never fail to make the balls tingle.'

'Sad, though, in a way. While they're showing their nipples to the waiters their host is sitting in a cell in Zarzuella jail.'

Hennessy laid a feather-light hand on my shoulder. 'Dear boy, I know. But Frank would be happy to see them here. He created the Club Nautico – it owes everything to him. Believe me, we've all been hoisting our piña coladas to him.'

I waited for Hennessy to remove his hand, so soft against my shirt that it might have belonged to the gentlest of importuning panders. Bland and sleek, with an openly ingratiating smile, he had cultivated a pleasant but vague manner that concealed, I suspected, a sophisticated kind of shiftiness. His eyes were always elsewhere when I tried to catch them. If the names in his Lloyd's syndicate had prospered, even that unlikely outcome would have had an ulterior motive. I was curious why this fastidious man had chosen the Costa del Sol, and found myself thinking of extradition treaties or, more exactly, their absence.

'I'm glad Frank was happy here. Estrella de Mar is the prettiest spot that I've seen on the coast. Still, I would have thought Palm Beach or Nassau more your style.'

Hennessy waved to a woman sunbathing in a pool-side lounger. 'Yes, friends at home used to say that to me. To be honest, I agreed with them when I first came here. But things have changed. This place isn't like anywhere else, you know. There's a very special atmosphere. Estrella de Mar is a real community. At times I think it's almost too lively.'

'Unlike the retirement complexes along the coast – Cala-honda and so on?'

'Absolutely. The people of the pueblos . . .' Hennessy averted his gaze from the poisoned coast. 'Brain-death disguised as a hundred miles of white cement. Estrella de Mar is more like Chelsea or Greenwich Village in the 1960s. There are theatre and film clubs, a choral society, cordon bleu classes. Some-times I dream of pure idleness, but not a hope. Stand still for a moment and you find yourself roped into a revival of *Waiting for Godot*.'

'I'm impressed. But what's the secret?'

'Let's say . . .' Hennessy checked himself, and let his smile drift across the air. 'It's something rather elusive. You have to find it for yourself. If you have time, do look around. I'm surprised you've never visited us before.'

'I should have done. But those tower blocks at Torremolinos throw long shadows. Without being snobbish, I assumed it was fish and chips, bingo and cheap sun-oil, all floating on a lake of lager. Not the sort of thing people want to read about in *The New Yorker*.'

'I dare say. Perhaps you'll write a friendly article about us?'

Hennessy was watching me in his affable way, but I sensed that a warning signal had sounded inside his head. He strolled into Frank's sitting room, shaking his head over the books pulled from the shelves during the police searches, as if enough rummaging had already taken place at Estrella de Mar.

'A friendly article?' I stepped over the scattered seat cushions. 'Perhaps . . . when Frank comes out. I need time to get my bearings.'

'Very sensible. You can't guess what you might find. Now, I'll drive you to the Hollingers'. I know you want to see the house. Be warned, though, you'll need to keep a strong grip on yourself.'

Hennessy waited as I made a last tour of the apartment. In Frank's bedroom the mattress stood against the wall, its seams slit by the police investigators searching for the smallest evidence that might corroborate his confession. Suits, shirts and sportswear lay strewn across the floor, and a lace shawl that had belonged to our mother hung over the dressing-table mirror. In the bathroom the hand-basin was filled with shaving gear, aerosols and vitamin packs swept from the shelves of the medicine cabinet. The bathtub was littered with broken glass, through which leaked a stream of blue shower gel.

On the sitting-room mantelpiece I recognized a childhood photograph of Frank and myself in Riyadh, standing with Mother outside our house in the residential compound. Frank's sly smile, and my owlish seriousness as the older brother, contrasted with our mother's troubled gaze as she strained to be cheerful for Father's camera. Curiously, the background of white villas, palms and apartment houses reminded me of Estrella de Mar.

Beside the row of tennis trophies was another framed photograph, taken by a professional cameraman in the dining room of the Club Nautico. Relaxed and pleasantly high, Frank was holding court in his white tuxedo among a group of his favourite members, the spirited blondes with deep *décolletages* and tolerant husbands.

Sitting beside Frank, hands clasped behind his head, was the fair-haired man I had seen on the tennis court. Frozen by the camera lens, he had the look of an intellectual athlete, his strong body offset by his fine-tuned features and sensitive gaze. He lounged back in his shirtsleeves, dinner jacket slung over a nearby chair, pleased with the happy scene around him but in some way above all this unthinking revelry. He struck me, as he must have done most people, as likeable but peculiarly driven.

'Your brother in jollier times,' Hennessy pointed to Frank. 'One of the theatre club dinners. Though photographs can be misleading – that was taken a week before the Hollinger fire.'

'And who's the brooding chap beside him? The club's leading Hamlet?'

'Far from it. Bobby Crawford, our tennis professional, though he's far more than that, I may say. You ought to meet him.'

'I did this afternoon.' I showed Hennessy the sticking-plaster which the concierge had pressed against my bleeding palm. 'I still have a piece of his tennis racket in my hand. I'm surprised he plays with a wooden one.'

'It slows down his game.' Hennessy seemed genuinely puzzled. 'How extraordinary. Were you on the courts with him? Bobby does play rather fiercely.'

J.G. Ballard

'Not with me. Though he was up against someone he couldn't quite beat.'

'Really? He's awfully good. Remarkable fellow in all sorts of ways. He's actually our entertainments officer, and the absolute life and soul of the Club Nautico. It was a brilliant coup of Frank's to bring him here – young Crawford's totally transformed the place. To be honest, before he came the club was pretty well dead. Like Estrella de Mar in many ways – we were turning into another dozy pueblo. Bobby threw himself into everything: fencing, drama, squash. He opened the disco downstairs, and he and Frank set up the Admiral Drake regatta. Forty years ago he'd have been running the Festival of Britain.'

'Perhaps he still is – he's certainly preoccupied with something. Yet he looks so young.'

'Ex-army man. The best junior officers stay young for ever. Strange about that splinter of yours . . .'

I was still trying to prise the splinter from my hand as I stared at the charred timbers of the Hollinger house. While Hennessy spoke to the Spanish chauffeur on the intercom I sat in the passenger seat beside him, glad that the windshield and the wrought-iron gates lay between me and the gutted mansion. The heat of the conflagration still seemed to radiate from the bruised hulk, which sat atop its hill like an ark put to the torch by a latter-day Noah. The roof joists jutted from the upper walls, a death-ship's exposed ribs topped by the masts of the chimneys. Scorched awnings hung from the windows like the shreds of sails, black flags flapping a sinister semaphore.

'Right – Miguel will let us in. He looks after the place, or what's left of it. The housekeeper and her husband have gone. They simply couldn't cope.' Hennessy waited for the gates to open. 'It's quite a spectacle, I must say . . .'

'What about the chauffeur – do I tell him that I'm Frank's brother? He may . . .'

'No. He liked Frank, sometimes they went scuba-diving together. He was very upset when Frank pleaded guilty. As we all were, needless to say.'

We entered the gates and rolled on to the thick gravel. The drive rose past a series of terraced gardens filled with miniature cycads, bougainvillea and frangipani. Sprinkler hoses ran across the hillside like the vessels of a dead blood system. Every leaf and flower was covered with white ash that bathed the derelict property in an almost sepulchral light. Footprints marked the ashy surface of the tennis court, as if a solitary player had waited after a brief snowfall for an absent opponent.

A marble terrace ran along the seaward frontage of the house, scattered with roof-tiles and charred sections of wooden gabling. Potted plants still bloomed among the overturned chairs and trestle tables. A large rectangular swimming pool sat like an ornamental reservoir beside the terrace, constructed in the 1920s, so Hennessy told me, to suit the tastes of the Andalucian tycoon who had bought the mansion. Marble pilasters supported the podium of the diving board, and each of the gargoyle spouts was a pair of carved stone hands that clasped an openmouthed fish. The filter system was silent, and the surface of the pool was covered with waterlogged timbers, floating wine bottles and paper cups, and a single empty ice-bucket.

Hennessy parked the car under a canopy of eucalyptus trees whose upper branches had been burned to blackened brooms. A young Spaniard with a sombre face climbed the steps from the pool, gazing at the devastation around him as if seeing it for the first time. I expected him to approach us, but he remained thirty feet away, staring at me stonily.

'Miguel, the Hollingers' chauffeur,' Hennessy murmured. 'He lives in the flat below the pool. A little tact might be in order if you ask any questions. The police gave him a hell of a time.'

J.G. Ballard

'Was he a suspect?'

'Who wasn't? Poor chap, his whole world literally fell in on him.'

Hennessy took off his hat and fanned himself as he gazed at the house. He seemed impressed by the scale of the disaster but otherwise unmoved, like an insurance assessor surveying a burned-out factory. He pointed to the yellow police tapes that sealed the embossed oak doors.

'Inspector Cabrera doesn't want anyone sifting through the evidence, though God only knows what's left. There's a side door off the terrace we can look through. It's too dangerous to go inside the place.'

I stepped over the shattered tiles and wine glasses at my feet. The intense heat had driven a jagged fissure through the stone walls, the scar of a lightning bolt that had condemned the property to the flames. Hennessy led the way towards a loose French door levered off its hinges by the firemen. Wind gusted across the terrace, and a cloud of white ash swirled around us like milled bone, restlessly hunting the air.

Hennessy pushed back the door and beckoned me towards him, smiling in a thin way like a guide at a black museum. A high-ceilinged drawing room looked out over the sea on either side of the peninsula. In the dim light I found myself standing in a marine world, the silt-covered state-room of a sunken liner. The Empire furniture and brocaded curtains, the tapestries and Chinese carpets were the decor of a drowned realm, drenched by the water that had poured through the collapsed ceiling. The dining room lay beyond the interior doors, where an oak table carried a pile of laths and plaster and the crystal debris of a chandelier.

I stepped from the parquet flooring on to the carpet, and found my shoes sinking as the water welled from the sodden fabric. Giving up, I returned to the terrace, where Hennessy was gazing at the sunlit peninsula.

'It's hard to believe one man started this fire,' I told him. 'Frank or anyone else. The place is completely gutted.'

'I agree.' Hennessy glanced at his watch, already keen to leave. 'Of course, this is a very old house. A single match would have set it going.'

The sounds of a tennis game echoed from a nearby court. A mile away I could make out the players at the Club Nautico, a glimmer of whites through the haze.

Where were the Hollingers found? I'm surprised they didn't run on to the terrace when the fire started.'

'Sadly, they were upstairs at the time.' Hennesy pointed to the blackened windows below the roof. 'He was in the bathroom next to his study. She was in another of the bedrooms.'

'This was when? About seven o'clock in the evening? What were they doing there?'

'Who can say? He was probably working on his memoirs. She might have been dressing for dinner. I'm sure they tried to escape, but the intense blaze and the ether fumes must have driven them back.'

I sniffed at the damp air, trying to catch a scent of the hospital corridors of my childhood, when I had visited my mother in the American clinic at Riyadh. The air in the drawing room carried the mould-like odours of a herb garden after a rain shower.

'Ether . . . ? There's something curious about that. Hospitals don't use ether any more. Where was Frank supposed to have bought all this bottled ether?'

Hennessy had moved away, watching me from a distance as if he had realized for the first time that I was a murderer's brother. Behind him Miguel stood among the overturned tables. Together they seemed like figures in a dream-play, trying to remind me of memories I could never recover.

'Ether?' Hennessy pondered this, moving aside a broken glass with one shoe. 'Yes. I suppose it does have industrial uses. Isn't it a good solvent? It must be available at specialist laboratories.'

'But why not use pure petrol? Or lighter fuel for that matter? No one would ever trace the stuff. I take it Cabrera tracked down the lab that's supposed to have sold this ether to Frank?'

'Perhaps, but I somehow doubt it. After all, your brother pleaded guilty.' Hennessy searched for his car keys. 'Charles, I think we ought to leave. You must find this a dreadful strain.'

'I'm fine. I'm glad you brought me here.' I pressed my hands against the stone balustrade, trying to feel the heat of the fire. 'Tell me about the others – the maid and the niece. There was a male secretary?'

'Roger Sansom, yes. Decent fellow, he'd been with them for years – almost a son.'

'Where were they found?'

'On the first floor. They were all in their bedrooms.'

'Isn't that a little odd? The fire started on the ground floor. You'd expect them to climb out through the windows. It's not that long a jump.'

'The windows would have been closed. The entire house was air-conditioned.' Hennessy tried to steer me across the terrace, a curator at closing time ushering a last visitor to the exit. 'We're all concerned for Frank, and absolutely mystified by the whole tragic business. But try to use a little imagination.'

'I'm probably using too much . . . I assume they were all identified?'

'With some difficulty. Dental records, I suppose, though I don't think either of the Hollingers had any teeth. Perhaps there are clues in the jawbone.'

'What were the Hollingers like? They were both in their seventies?'

'He was seventy-five. She was quite a bit younger. Late sixties, I imagine.' Hennessy smiled to himself, as if fondly remembering a choice wine. 'Good-looking woman, in an actressy way, though a little too ladylike for me.'

'And they came here twenty years ago? Estrella de Mar must have been very different then.'

'There was nothing to see, just bare hillsides and a few old vines. A collection of fishermen's shacks and a small bar. Hollinger bought the house from a Spanish property developer he worked with. Believe me, it was a beautiful place.'

'And I can imagine how the Hollingers felt as all this cement crawled up the hill towards them. Were they popular here? Hollinger was rich enough to put a spoke into a lot of wheels.'

'They were fairly popular. We didn't see too much of them at the club, though Hollinger was a major investor. I suspect they assumed it was going to be for their exclusive use.'

'But then the gold medallions started to arrive?'

'I don't think they worried about gold medallions. Gold was one of Hollinger's favourite colours. Estrella de Mar had begun to change. He and Alice were more put off by the art galleries and the Tom Stoppard revivals. They kept to themselves. In fact, I believe he was trying to sell his interest in the club.'

Hennessy reluctantly followed me along the terrace. A narrow balcony circled the house and led to a stone staircase that climbed the hillside fifty feet away. A grove of lemon trees had once filled the bedroom windows with their oily scent, but the fire-storm had driven through them, and now only the charred stumps rose from the ground like a forest of black umbrellas.

'Good God, there's a fire escape . . .' I pointed to the cast-iron steps that descended from a doorway on the first floor. The massive structure had been warped by the heat, but still clung to the stone walls. 'Why didn't they use this? They would have been safe in seconds.'

Hennessy removed his hat in a gesture of respect for the victims. He stood with his head bowed before speaking. 'Charles, they never left their bedrooms. The fire was too intense. The whole house was a furnace.'

J.G. Ballard

'I can see that. Your local fire brigade didn't even begin to get it under control. Who alerted them, by the way?'

Hennessy seemed hardly to have heard me. He turned his back on the house, and gazed at the sea. I sensed that he was telling me only what he knew I would learn elsewhere.

'As a matter of fact, the alarm was raised by a passing motorist. No one called the fire services from here.'

'And the police?'

'They didn't arrive until an hour later. You have to understand that the Spanish police leave us very much to ourselves. Few crimes are ever reported in Estrella de Mar. We have our own security patrols and they keep an eye on things.'

'The police and fire services were called only later...' I repeated this to myself, visualizing the arsonist making his escape across the deserted terrace and then climbing the outer wall as the flames roared through the great roof. 'So, apart from the housekeeper and her husband there was no one here?'

'Not exactly.' Hennessy replaced his hat, lowering the brim over his eyes. 'As it happens, everyone was here.'

'Everyone? Do you mean the staff?'

'No, I mean...' Hennessy gestured with his pale hands at the town below. '*Le tout* Estrella de Mar. It was the Queen's birthday. The Hollingers always threw a party for the club members. It was their contribution to community life – a touch of noblesse oblige about it, I have to admit, but they were rather nice shows. Champagne and excellent canapés...'

I cupped my hands and stared at the Club Nautico, visualizing the entire membership decamping to the Hollinger mansion for the loyal toast. 'The fire took place on the night of the party ... that was why the club had closed. How many people were actually here when it started?'

'Everyone. I think all the guests had arrived. I suppose there were about ... two hundred of us.'

'Two hundred people?' I walked back to the south face of the house, where the balcony overlooked the swimming pool and terrace. I imagined the trestle tables decked in white cloths, the ice-buckets gleaming in the evening lights, and the guests chattering beside the unruffled water. 'There were all these people here, at least two hundred of them, and no one entered the house and tried to save the Hollingers?'

'Dear boy, the doors were locked.'

'At a party? I don't get it. You could have broken in.'

'Security glass. The house was filled with paintings and *objets d'art*, not to mention Alice's jewellery. In previous years there'd been pilfering and cigarette burns on the carpets.'

'Even so. Besides, what were the Hollingers doing indoors? Why weren't they out here mingling with their guests?'

'The Hollingers weren't the mingling type.' Hennessy gestured patiently. 'They'd greet a few old friends, but I don't think they ever joined the other guests. It was all rather regal. They kept an eye on things from the first-floor veranda. Hollinger proposed the Queen's toast from there, and Alice would wave and acknowledge the cheers.'

We had reached the swimming pool, where Miguel was raking the floating debris from the water at the shallow end. Piles of wet charcoal lay on the marble verge. The ice-bucket floated past us, an unravelled cigar inside it.

'David, I can't understand all this. The whole thing seems . . .' I waited until Hennessy was forced to meet my eyes. 'Two hundred people are standing by a swimming pool when a fire starts. There are ice-buckets, punchbowls, bottles of champagne and mineral water, enough to dowse a volcano. But no one seems to have moved a finger. That's the eerie thing. No one called the police or fire brigade. What did you do – just stand here?'

Hennessy had begun to tire of me, his gaze fixed on his car. 'What else was there to do? There was tremendous panic, people

J.G. Ballard

were falling into the pool and running off in all directions. No one had time to think of the police.'

'And what about Frank? Was he here?'

'Very much so. We stood together during the Queen's toast. After that he started circulating, as he always does. I can't be sure I saw him again.'

'But in the minutes before the fire started? Tell me, did anyone see Frank light the fire?'

'Of course not. It's unthinkable.' Hennessy turned to stare at me. 'For heaven's sake, old chap, Frank is your brother.'

'But he was found with a bottle of ether in his hands. Didn't it strike you as a little odd?'

'That was three or four hours later, when the police arrived at the club. It may have been planted in his apartment, who knows?' Hennessy patted my shoulders, as if reassuring a disappointed member of his Lloyd's syndicate. 'Look, Charles, give yourself time to take it all in. Talk to as many people as you want – they'll all tell you the same story, appalling as it is. No one thinks Frank was responsible, but at the same time it's not clear who else could have started the fire.'

I waited for him as he walked around the pool and spoke to Miguel. A few banknotes changed hands, which the Spaniard slipped into his pocket with a grimace of distaste. Rarely taking his eyes from me, he followed us on foot as we drove past the ash-covered tennis court. I sensed that he wanted to speak to me, but he operated the gate controls without a word, a faint tic jumping across his scarred cheek.

'Unnerving fellow,' I commented as we rolled away. 'Tell me, was Bobby Crawford at the party? The tennis professional?'

For once Hennessy answered promptly. 'No, he wasn't. He stayed behind at the club, playing tennis with that machine of his. I don't think he cared overmuch for the Hollingers. Nor they for him . . .'

★ ★ ★

Hennessy returned us to the Club Nautico, and left me with the keys to Frank's apartment. When we parted at the door of his office he was clearly glad to be rid of me, and I guessed that I was already becoming a mild embarrassment to the club and its members. Yet he knew that Frank could not have started the fire or taken even the smallest role in the conspiracy to kill the Hollingers. The confession, however preposterous, had stopped the clock, and no one seemed able to think beyond his guilty plea to the far larger question mark that presided over the gutted mansion.

I spent the afternoon tidying Frank's apartment. I replaced the books on the shelves, remade the bed and straightened the dented lampshades. The grooves in the sitting-room rugs indicated where the sofa, easy chairs and desk had stood before the police search. Pushing them back into place, I felt like a props man on a darkened stage, preparing the scene for the next day's performance.

The castors settled into their familiar ruts, but little else in Frank's world fitted together. I hung his scattered shirts in the wardrobe, and carefully folded the antique lace shawl in which we had both been wrapped as babies. After our mother's death Frank had retrieved the shawl from the bundle of clothes that Father had consigned to a Riyadh charity. The ancient fabric, inherited from his grandmother, was as grey and delicate as a folded cobweb.

I sat at Frank's desk, flicking through his cheque-book stubs and credit-card receipts, hoping for a pointer to his involvement with the Hollingers. The drawers were filled with a clutter of old wedding invitations, insurance renewal notices, holiday postcards from friends, French and English coins, and a health passport with its out-of-date tetanus and typhoid vaccinations, the trivia of everyday life that we shed like our skins.

Surprisingly, Inspector Cabrera's men had missed a small sachet of cocaine tucked into an envelope filled with foreign stamps that Frank had torn from his overseas mail and was evidently collecting for a colleague's child. I fingered the plastic sachet, tempted to help myself to this forgotten cache, but I was too unsettled by the visit to the Hollinger house.

In the centre drawer was an old photographic album that Mother had kept as a girl in Bognor Regis. Its chocolate-box covers and marbled pages with their art nouveau frames seemed as remote as the Charleston and the Hispano-Suiza. The black and white snaps showed an over-eager little girl trying hopelessly to build a pebble castle on a shingle beach, beaming shyly by her father's side and pinning the tail on a donkey at a birthday party. The flat sunless world was an ominous start for a child so clearly straining to be happy, and scant preparation for her marriage to an ambitious young historian and Arabist. Prophetically, the collection came to a sudden end a year after her arrival at Riyadh, as if the blank pages said everything about her growing depression.

After a quiet dinner in the deserted restaurant I fell asleep on the sofa, the album across my chest, and woke after midnight as a boisterous party spilled from the disco on to the terrace of the swimming pool. Two men in white dinner jackets were splashing across the pool, wine glasses raised to toast their wives, who were stripping to their underwear beside the diving board. A drunken young woman in a gold sheath dress tottered along the verge, snatched off her stiletto shoes and hurled them into the water.

Frank's absence had liberated his members, transforming the Club Nautico into an intriguing mix of casino and bordello. When I left the apartment to return to Los Monteros an amorous couple were testing the locked doors in the corridor. Almost all the staff had left for home, and the restaurant and bridge rooms were in darkness, but strobe lights from the disco veered across the entrance. Three young women stood on the steps, dressed like amateur whores in micro-skirts, fishnet tights and scarlet bustiers. I guessed that they were members of the club on the way to a costume party, and was tempted to offer them a lift, but they were busily checking a list of telephone numbers.

The car park was unlit, and I blundered among the lines of vehicles, feeling for the door latch of the rented Renault. Sitting behind the wheel, I listened to the boom of the disco drumming at the night. In a Porsche parked nearby a large white dog was jumping across the seats, unsettled by the noise and eager to see its owner.

I searched the shroud of the steering column for the ignition switch. When my eyes sharpened I realized that the dog was a man in a cream tuxedo, struggling with someone he had pinned against the passenger seat. In the brief pause between the disco numbers I heard a woman's shout, little more than an exhausted gasp. Her hands reached to the roof above the man's head and tore at the fabric.

Twenty feet away from me a rape was taking place. I switched on the headlamps and sounded three long blasts on the horn. As I stepped on to the gravel the Porsche's door sprang open, striking the vehicle beside it. The would-be rapist leapt from the car, the tuxedo almost stripped from his back by the frantic victim. He swerved away through the darkness, leaping between the Renault's headlamps. I ran after him, but he raced across the knoll beside the gates, straightened the tuxedo with a careless shrug, and vanished into the night.

The woman sat in the passenger seat of the Porsche, her bare feet protruding through the door, skirt around her waist. Her blonde hair gleamed with the attacker's saliva, and her blurred lipstick gave her a child's jamjar face. She pulled her torn underwear up her thighs and retched on to the gravel, then reached into the back seat and retrieved her shoes, brushing the torn roof liner from her face.

A few steps away was the booth from which the parking

attendant kept watch on his charges during the day and evening. I leaned across the counter and snapped down the master switch of the lighting system, flooding the car park with a harsh fluorescence.

The woman frowned at the sudden glare, hid her eyes behind a silver purse and hobbled on a broken heel towards the entrance of the club, creased skirt over her ripped tights.

'Wait!' I shouted to her. 'I'll call the police for you . . .'

I was about to follow her when I noticed the row of parked cars that faced the Porsche across the access lane. Several of the front seats were occupied by the drivers and their passengers, all in evening dress, faces concealed by the lowered sun vizors. They had watched the rape attempt without intervening, like a gallery audience at an exclusive private view.

'What are you people playing at?' I shouted. 'For God's sake . . .'

I walked towards them, angry that they had failed to save the bruised woman, and drummed my bandaged fist on the windshields. But the drivers had started their engines. Following each other, they swerved past me towards the gates, the women shielding their eyes behind their hands.

I returned to the club, trying to find the victim of the assault. The fancy-dress whores stood in the lobby, phone lists in hand, but turned towards me as I strode up the steps.

'Where is she?' I called to them. 'She was damn nearly raped out there. Did you see her come in?'

The three gazed wide-eyed at each other, and then began to giggle together, minds slewing across some crazed amphetamine space. One of them touched my cheek, as if calming a child.

I searched the women's rest-room, kicking back the doors of the cubicles, and then blundered through the tables of the darkened restaurant, trying to catch the scent of heliotrope that the woman had left on the night air. At last I saw her beside the pool, dancing shoeless on the flooded grass, the backs of her hands smeared with lipstick, smiling at me in a knowing way when I walked towards her and tried to take her arm.

William Burroughs

Naked Lunch

'A true genius and first mythographer of the mid-twentieth century, William Burroughs is the lineal successor to James Joyce. *Naked Lunch* is a banquet you will never forget.'

J.G. BALLARD

William Burroughs was born in St Louis, Missouri, in 1914. Although largely unpublished for many years, he was immensely influential among the Beat writers of the 1950s – notably Jack Kerouac and Allen Ginsberg – and already had an underground reputation before the appearance of his first important book, the provocative, morbidly fascinating collage of addiction and sexual violence that is *Naked Lunch*. First published in France in 1959, it aroused great controversy on publication and was not available in the UK until 1964.

Burroughs' other works include *The Soft Machine, The Ticket That Exploded, Nova Express* and the confessional books *Junky* and *Queer*, the latter of which was written in the 1950s but not published until 1985. He divided his time between New York and Lawrence, Kansas, until his death in 1997.

Flamingo publishes a Burroughs selection (including previously unpublished material), *Word Virus*, in October 1999.

Naked Lunch
Available now from Flamingo
ISBN 0 586 08560 2

The Market

PANORAMA OF THE City of Interzone. Opening bars of East St Louis Toodleoo . . . at times loud and clear then faint and intermittent like music down a windy street . . .

The room seems to shake and vibrate with motion. The blood and substance of many races, Negro, Polynesian, Mountain Mongol, Desert Nomad, Polyglot Near East, Indian – races as yet unconceived and unborn, combinations not yet realized pass through your body. Migrations, incredible journeys through deserts and jungles and mountains (stasis and death in closed mountain valleys where plants grow out of genitals, vast crustaceans hatch inside and break the shell of body) across the Pacific in an outrigger canoe to Easter Island. The Composite City where all human potentials are spread out in a vast silent market.

Minarets, palms, mountains, jungle . . . A sluggish river jumping with vicious fish, vast weed-grown parks where boys lie in the grass, play cryptic games. Not a locked door in the City. Anyone comes into your room at any time. The Chief of Police is a Chinese who picks his teeth and listens to denunciations presented by a lunatic. Every now and then the Chinese takes the toothpick out of his mouth and looks at the end of it. Hipsters with smooth copper-coloured faces lounge in doorways twisting shrunken heads on gold chains, their faces blank with an insect's unseeing calm.

Behind them, through open doors, tables and booths and

bars, and kitchens and baths, copulating couples on rows of brass beds, crisscross of a thousand hammocks, junkies typing up for a shot, opium smokers, hashish smokers, people eating talking bathing back into a haze of smoke and steam.

Gaming tables where the games are played for incredible stakes. From time to time a player leaps up with a despairing cry, having lost his youth to an old man or become Latah to his opponent. But there are higher stakes than youth or Latah, games where only two players in the world know what the stakes are.

All houses in the City are joined. Houses of sod – high mountain Mongols blink in smokey doorways – houses of bamboo and teak, houses of adobe, stone and red brick, South Pacific and Maori houses, houses in trees and river boats, wood houses one hundred feet long sheltering entire tribes, houses of boxes and corrugated iron where old men sit in rotten rags cooking down canned heat, great rusty iron racks rising two hundred feet in the air from swamps and rubbish with perilous partitions built on multi-levelled platforms, and hammocks swinging over the void.

Expeditions leave for unknown places with unknown pur-poses. Strangers arrive on rafts of old packing crates tied together with rotten rope, they stagger in out of the jungle their eyes swollen shut from insect bites, they come down the mountain trails on cracked bleeding feet through the dusty windy outskirts of the city, where people defecate in rows along adobe walls and vultures fight over fish heads. They drop down into parks in patched parachutes . . . They are escorted by a drunken cop to register in a vast public lavatory. The data taken down is put on pegs to be used as toilet paper.

Cooking smells of all countries hang over the City, a haze of opium, hashish, the resinous red smoke of Yage, smell of the jungle and salt water and the rotting river and dried excre-ment and sweat and genitals.

High mountain flutes, jazz and bebop, one-stringed Mongol instruments, gypsy xylophones, African drums, Arab bagpipes . . .

The City is visited by epidemics of violence, and the untended dead are eaten by vultures in the streets. Albinos blink in the sun. Boys sit in trees, languidly masturbate. People eaten by unknown diseases watch the passerby with evil, knowing eyes.

In the City Market is the Meet Café. Followers of obsolete, unthinkable trades doodling in Etruscan, addicts of drugs not yet synthesized, pushers of souped-up Harmaline, junk reduced to pure habit offering precarious vegetable serenity, liquids to induce Latah, Tithonian longevity serums, black marketeers of World War III, excisors of telepathic sensitivity, osteopaths of the spirit, investigators of infractions denounced by bland paranoid chess players, servers of fragmentary warrants taken down in hebephrenic shorthand charging unspeakable mutilations of the spirit, bureaucrats of spectral departments, officials of unconstituted police states, a Lesbian dwarf who has perfected operation Bangutot, the lung erection that strangles a sleeping enemy, sellers of orgone tanks and relaxing machines, brokers of exquisite dreams and memories tested on the sensitized cells of junk sickness and bartered for raw materials of the will, doctors skilled in the treatment of diseases dormant in the black dust of ruined cities, gathering virulence in the white blood of eyeless worms feeling slowly to the surface and the human host, maladies of the ocean floor and the stratosphere, maladies of the laboratory and atomic war . . . A place where the unknown past and the emergent future meet in a vibrating soundless hum . . . Larval entities waiting for a Live One . . .

(Section describing The City and the Meet Café written in state of Yage intoxication . . . Yage, Ayuahuasca, Pilde, Nateema are Indian names for Bannisteria Caapi, a fast growing vine indigenous to the Amazon region. See discussion of Yage in Appendix.)

Notes from Yage state: Images fall slow and silent like snow . . . Serenity . . . All defenses fall . . . everything is free to enter or to go out . . . Fear is simply impossible . . . A beautiful blue substance flows into me . . . I see an archaic grinning face like South Pacific mask . . . The face is blue purple splotched with gold . . .

The room takes on aspect of Near East whorehouse with blue walls and red tasseled lamps . . . I feel myself turning into a Negress, the black colour silently invading my flesh . . . Convulsions of lust . . . My legs take on a well rounded Polynesian substance . . . Everything stirs with a writhing furtive life . . . The room is Near East, Negro, South Pacific, in some familiar place I cannot locate . . . Yage is space-time travel . . . The room seems to shake and vibrate with motion . . . The blood and substance of many races, Negro, Polynesian, Mountain Mongol, Desert Nomad, Polyglot Near East, Indian, races as yet unconceived and unborn, passes through the body . . . Migrations, incredible journeys through deserts and jungles and mountains (stasis and death in closed mountain valley where plants grow out of genitals, vast crustaceans hatch inside and break the shell of body) across the Pacific in an outrigger canoe to Easter Island . . .

(It occurs to me that preliminary Yage nausea is motion sickness of transport to Yage state . . .)

'All medicine men use it in their practice to foretell the future, locate lost or stolen objects, to diagnose and treat illness, to name the perpetrator of a crime.' Since the Indian (straitjacket for Herr Boas – trade joke – nothing so maddens an anthropologist as Primitive Man) does not regard any death as accidental, and they are unacquainted with their own self-destructive trends referring to them contemptuously as 'our naked cousins,' or perhaps feeling that these trends above all are subject to the manipulation of alien and hostile wills, any death is murder. The medicine man takes Yage and the identity of the murderer is revealed to him. As you may imagine, the deliberations of the medicine man during one of these jungle inquests give rise to certain feelings of uneasiness among his constituents.

'Let's hope Old Xiuptutol don't wig and name one of the boys.'

'Take a curare and relax. We got the fix in . . .'

'But if he *wig*? Picking up on that Nateema all the time he don't touch the ground in twenty years . . . I tell you, Boss, nobody can hit the stuff like that . . . It cooks the brains . . .'

'So we declare him incompetent . . .'

So Xiuptutol reels out of the jungle and says the boys in the Lower Tzpino territory done it, which surprises no one . . . Take it from an old Brujo, dearie, they don't like surprises . . .

A funeral passes through the market. Black coffin – Arabic inscriptions in filigreed silver – carried by four pallbearers. Procession of mourners singing the funeral song . . . Clem and Jody fall in beside them carrying coffin, the corpse of a hog bursts out of it . . . The hog is dressed in a jellaba, a keif pipe juts from its mouth, one hoof holds a packet of feelthy pictures, a mezuzzoth hangs about its neck . . . Inscribed on the coffin: 'This was the noblest Arab of them all.'

They sing hideous parody of the funeral song in false Arabic. Jody can do a fake Chinese spiel that'll just kill you – like a hysterical ventriloquist's dummy. In fact, he precipitated an anti-foreign riot in Shanghai that claimed 3,000 casualties.

'Stand up, Gertie, and show respect for the local gooks.'

'I suppose one *should*.'

'My dear, I'm working on the most marvellous invention . . . a boy who disappears as soon as you come leaving a smell of burning leaves and a sound effect of distant train whistles.'

'Ever make sex in no gravity? Your jism just floats out in the air like lovely ectoplasm, and female guests are subject to immaculate or at least indirect conception . . . Reminds me of an old friend of mine, one of the handsomest men I have ever known and one of the maddest and absolutely ruined by wealth. He used to go about with a water pistol shooting jism up career women at parties. Won all his paternity suits hands down. Never use his own jism you understand.'

Fadeout . . . 'Order in the Court.' Attorney for A. J., 'Conclusive tests have established that my client has no uh personal connection with the uh little accident to the charming plaintiff . . . Perhaps she is preparing to emulate the Virgin Mary and conceive immaculately naming my client as a harumph ghostly panderer . . . I am reminded of a case in fifteenth-century Holland where a young woman accused an elderly and respectable sorcerer of conjuring up a succubus who then had uh carnal knowledge of the young person in question with the under the circumstances regrettable result of pregnancy. So the sorcerer was indicted as an accomplice and rampant voyeur before during and after the fact. However, gentlemen of the jury, we no longer credit such uh legends; and a young woman attributing her uh interesting condition to the attentions of a succubus would be accounted, in these enlightened days, a romanticist or in plain English a God damned liar hehe hehe heh . . .'

And now The Prophet's Hour:

'Millins died in the mud flats. Only one blast free to lungs.

'"Eye Eye, Captain," he said, squirting his eyes out on the deck . . . And who would put on the chains tonight? It is indicated to observe some caution in the upwind approach, the down wind having failed to turn up anything worth a rusty load . . . Señoritas are the wear this season in Hell, and I am tired with the long climb to a pulsing Vesuvius of alien pricks.'

Need Orient Express out of here to no hide place(r) mines are frequent in the area . . . Every day dig a little it takes up the time . . .

　　　　　　　　　　　　　　　　William Burroughs

Jack of phantoms whisper hot into the bone ear . . .

Shoot your way to freedom.

'*Christ*?' sneers the vicious, fruity old Saint applying pancake from an alabaster bowl . . . 'That cheap ham! You think I'd demean myself to commit a miracle? . . . That one should have stood in carny . . .

' "Step right up, Marquesses and Marks, and bring the little Marks too. Good for young and old, man and beast . . . The one and only legit *Son of Man* will cure a young boy's clap with one hand – by contact alone, folks – create marijuana with the other, whilst walking on water and squirting wine out of his ass . . . Now keep your distance, folks, you is subject to be irradiated by the sheer charge of this character."

'And I knew him when, dearie . . . I recall we was doing an Impersonation Act – very high class too – in Sodom, and that is one cheap town . . . Strictly from hunger . . . Well, this citizen, this fucking Philistine wandered in from Podunk Baal or some place, called me a fucking fruit right on the floor. And I said to him: "Three thousand years in show business and I always keep my nose clean. Besides I don't hafta take any shit off any uncircumcised cocksucker." . . . Later he come to my dressing room and made an apology . . . Turns out he is a big physician. And he was a lovely fellah, too . . .

'*Buddha*? A notorious metabolic junky . . . Makes his own you dig. In India, where they got no sense of time, The Man is often a month late . . . "Now let me see, is that the second or the third monsoon? I got like a meet in Ketchupore about more or less."

'And all them junkies sitting around in the lotus posture spitting on the ground and waiting on The Man.

'So Buddha says: "I don't hafta take this sound. I'll by God metabolize my own junk."

' "Man you can't do that. The Revenooers will swarm all over you."

' "Over me they won't swarm. I gotta gimmick, see? I'm a fuckin Holy Man as of right now."

' "Jeez, boss, what an angle."

' "Now some citizens really wig when they make with the New Religion. These frantic individuals do not know how to come on. No class to them . . . Besides, they is subject to be lynched like who wants somebody hanging around being better'n other folks? 'What you trying to do, Jack, give people a bad time? . . .' So we gotta play it cool, you dig, cool . . . We got a take it or leave it proposition here, folks. We don't shove anything up your soul, unlike certain cheap characters who shall be nameless and are nowhere. Clear the cave for action. I'm gonna metabolize a speed ball and make with the Fire Sermon."

'*Mohammed*? Are you kidding? He was dreamed up by the Mecca Chamber of Commerce. An Egyptian ad man on the skids from the sauce write the continuity.

' "I'll have one more, Gus. Then, by Allah, I will go home and receive a Surah . . . Wait'll the morning edition hits the souks. I am blasting Amalgamated Images wide open."

'The bartender looks up from his racing form. "Yeah. And theirs will be a painful doom."

' "Oh . . . uh . . . quite. Now, Gus, I'll write you a check."

' "You are only being the most notorious paper hanger in Greater Mecca. I am not a wall, Mr Mohammed."

' "Well, Gus, I got like two types publicity, favourable and otherwise. You want some otherwise already? I am subject to receive a Surah concerning bartenders who extendeth not credit to those in a needy way."

' "And theirs will be a painful doom. Sold Arabia." He vaults over the bar. "I'm not taking any more, Ahmed. Pick up thy Surahs and walk. In fact, I'll help you. And *stay out*."

' "I'll fix your wagon good, you unbelieving cocksucker. I'll close you up tight and dry as a junky's asshole. I'll by Allah dry up the Peninsula."

' "It's a continent already . . ."'

'Leave what Confucius say stand with Little Audrey and the shaggy dogs. Lao-Tze? They scratch him already . . . And enough of these gooey saints with a look of pathic dismay as if they getting fucked up the ass and try not to pay any mind. And why should we let some old brokendown ham tell us what wisdom is? "Three thousand years in show business and I always keep my nose clean . . ."'

'First, every Fact is incarcerate along with the male hustlers and those who desecrate the gods of commerce by playing ball in the streets, and some old white-haired fuck staggers out to give us the benefits of his ripe idiocy. Are we never to be free of this grey-beard loon lurking on every mountain top in Tibet, subject to drag himself out of a hut in the Amazon, waylay one in the Bowery? "I've been expecting you, my son," And he make with a silo full of corn. "Life is a school where every pupil must learn a different lesson. And now I will unlock my Word Hoard . . ."'

' "I do fear it much."'

' "Nay, nothing shall stem the rising tide."'

' "I can't stem him, boys. *Sauve qui peut.*"'

' "I tell you when I leave the Wise Man I don't even feel like a human. He converting my life orgones into dead bullshit."'

'So I got an exclusive why don't I make with the live word? The word cannot be expressed direct . . . It can perhaps be indicated by mosaic of juxtaposition like articles abandoned in a hotel drawer, defined by negatives and absence . . .

'Think I'll have my stomach tucked . . . I may be old, but I'm still desirable.'

(The Stomach Tuck is surgical intervention to remove stomach fat at the same time making a tuck in the abdominal wall, thus creating a Flesh Corset, which is, however, subject to break and spurt your horrible old guts across the floor . . . The slim and shapely F.C. models are, of course, the most dangerous. In fact, some extreme models are known as O.N.S. – One Night Stands – in the industry.

Doctor 'Doodles' Rinderpest states bluntly: 'Bed is the most dangerous place for an F.C. man.'

The F.C. theme song is 'Believe Me If All These Endearing Young Charms.' An F.C. partner is indeed subject to 'flee from your arms like fairy gifts fading away.'

In a white museum room full of sunlight pink nudes sixty feet high. Vast adolescent muttering.

Silver guard rail . . . chasm a thousand feet down into the glittering sunlight. Little green plots of cabbage and lettuce. Brown youths with adzes spied by the old queen across a sewage canal.

'Oh dear, I wonder if they fertilize with human excrement . . . Maybe they'll do it now.'

He flips out mother of pearl opera glasses – Aztec mosaic in the sun.

Long line of Greek lads march up with alabaster bowels of shit, empty into the limestone marl hole.

Dusty poplars shake across the red brick Plaza de Toros in the afternoon wind.

Wooden cubicles around a hot spring . . . rubble of ruined walls in a grove of cottonwoods . . . the benches worn smooth as metal by a million masturbating boys.

Greek lads white as marble fuck dog style on the portico of a great golden temple . . . naked Mugwump twangs a lute.

Walking down by the tracks in his red sweater met Sammy the Dock Keeper's son with two Mexicans.

'Hey, Skinny,' he said, 'want to get screwed?'

'Well . . . Yeah.'

On a ruined straw mattress the Mexican pulled him up on all fours – Negro boy dance around them beating out the strokes . . . sun through a knot-hole pink spotlights his cock.

A waste of raw pink shame to the pastel blue horizon where vast iron mesas crash into the shattered sky.

'It's all right.' The God screams through you three thousand year rusty load . . .

Hail of crystal skulls shattered the greenhouse to slivers in the winter moon . . .

The American woman has left a whiff of poison behind in the dank St Louis garden party.

Pool covered with green slime in a ruined French garden. Huge pathic frog rises slowly from the water on a mud platform playing the clavichord.

A Sollubi rushes into the bar and starts polishing The Saint's shoes with the oil on his nose . . . The Saint kicks him petulantly in the mouth. The Sollubi screams, whirls around and shits on the Saint's pants. Then he dashes into the street. A pimp looks after him speculatively . . .

The Saint calls the manager: 'Jesus, Al, what kinda creep joint you running here? My brand new fishskin Dégagées . . .'

'I'm sorry, Saint. He slipped by me.'

(The Sollubi are an untouchable caste in Arabia noted for their abject vileness. De luxe cafés are equipped with Sollubi who rim the guests while they eat − holes in the seating benches being provided for this purpose. Citizens who want to be utterly humiliated and degraded − so many people do nowadays, hoping to jump the gun − offer themselves up for passive homosexual intercourse to an encampment of Sollubis . . . Nothing like it, they tell me . . . In fact, the Sollubi are subject to become wealthy and arrogant and lose their native vileness. What is origin of untouchable? Perhaps a fallen priest caste. In fact, untouchables perform a priestly function in taking on themselves all human vileness.

A. J. strolls through the Market in black cape with a vulture perched on one shoulder. He stands by a table of agents.

'This you gotta hear. Boy in Los Angeles fifteen year old. Father decide it is time the boy have his first piece of ass. Boy is lying on the lawn reading comic books, father go out and say: "Son here's twenty dollars: I want you to go to a good whore and get a piece of ass off her."

'So they drive to this plush jump joint and the father say, "All right, son. You're on your own. So ring the bell and when the woman come give her the twenty dollars and tell her you want a piece of ass."

'"Solid, pop."

'So about fifteen minutes later the boy comes out:

'"Well, son, did you get a piece of ass?"

'"Yeah. This gash comes to the door, and I say I want a piece of ass and lay the double sawski on her. We go up to her trap, and she remove the dry goods. So I switch my blade and cut a big hunk off her ass, she raise a beef like I am reduce to pull off one shoe and beat her brains out. Then I hump her for kicks.'

Only the laughing bones remain, flesh over the hills and far away with the dawn wind and a train whistle. We are not unaware of the problem, and the needs of our constituents are never out of our mind being their place of residence and who can break a ninety-nine year synapses lease?

Another instalment in the adventures of Clem Snide the Private Ass Hole: 'So I walk in the joint, and this female hustler sit at the bar, and I think, "Oh God, you're poule de luxe already." I mean it's like I see the gash before. So I don't pay her no mind at first, then I dig she is rubbing her legs together and working her feet up behind her head shoves it down to give herself a douche job with a gadget sticks out of her nose the way a body can't help but notice.'

Iris – half Chinese and half Negro – addicted to dihydro-oxyheroin – takes a shot every fifteen minutes to which end she leaves droppers and needles sticking out all over her. The needles rust in her dry flesh, which, here and there, has grown completely over a joint to form a smooth green brown wen. On the table in front of her is a samovar of tea and a twenty-pound hamper of brown sugar. No one has ever seen her eat anything else. It is only just before a shot that she hears what anyone says or talks herself. Then she makes some flat, factual statement relative to her own person.

'My asshole is occluding.'

'My cunt got terrible green juices.'

Iris is one of Benway's projects. 'The human body can run on sugar alone, God damn it . . . I am aware that certain of my learned colleagues, who are attempting to belittle my genius work, claim that I put vitamins and proteins into Iris's sugar clandestinely . . . I challenge these nameless assholes to crawl up out of their latrines and run a spot analysis on Iris's sugar and her tea. Iris is a wholesome American cunt. I deny categorically that she nourishes herself on semen. And let me take this opportunity to state that I am a reputable scientist, not a charlatan, a lunatic, or a pretended worker of miracles . . . I never claimed that Iris could subsist exclusive on photosynthesis . . . I did not say she could breathe in carbon dioxide and give off oxygen – I confess I have been tempted to experiment being of course restrained by my medical ethics . . . In short, the vile slanders of my creeping opponents will inevitably fall back onto them and come to roost like a homing stool pigeon.'

Douglas Coupland

Microserfs

'A funny and stridently topical novel. Coupland continues to register the buzz of his generation.'

JAY McINERNEY, *New York Times*

At computer giant Microsoft, Dan, Susan, Abe, Todd and Bug are struggling to get a life in a high-speed, high-tech environment. The job may be super cool, the pay may be astronomical, but they're heading nowhere, and however hard they work, however many shares they earn, they're never going to be as rich as Bill. And besides, with all the hours they're putting in, their best relationships are on e-mail. Something's got to give . . .

———————

Douglas Coupland was born on 30 December 1961 on a Canadian NATO base in Germany. He grew up and lives in Vancouver, Canada. His other books include *Generation X, Shampoo Planet, Polaroids from the Dead* and, most recently, *Girlfriend in a Coma*.

Flamingo publishes Douglas Coupland's new novel, *Miss Wyoming*, in February 2000.

Microserfs
Available now from Flamingo
ISBN 0 00 654859 8

Saturday

Shipping hell continued again today. Grind, grind, grind. We'll never make it. Have I said that already? Why do we always underestimate our shipping schedules? I just don't understand. In at 9:30 a.m.; out at 11:30 p.m. Domino's for dinner. And three diet Cokes.

I got bored a few times today and checked the WinQuote on my screen – that's the extension that gives continuous updates on Microsoft's NASDAQ price. It was Saturday, and there was never any change, but I kept forgetting. Habit. Maybe the Tokyo or Hong Kong exchanges might cause a fluctuation?

Most staffers peek at WinQuote a few times a day. I mean, if you have 10,000 shares (and tons of staff members have way more) and the stock goes up a buck, you've just made ten grand! But then, if it goes down two dollars, you've just lost twenty grand. It's a real psychic yo-yo. Last April Fool's Day, someone fluctuated the price up and down by fifty dollars and half the staff had coronaries.

Because I started out low on the food chain and worked my way up, I didn't get much stock offered to me the way that programmers and systems designers get stock firehosed onto them when they start. What stock I do own won't fully vest for another 2.5 years (stock takes 4.5 years to fully vest).

Susan's stock vests later this week, and she's going to have a vesting party. And then she's going to quit. Larger social forces are at work, threatening to dissolve our group house.

The stock closed up $1.75 on Friday. Bill has 78,000,000 shares, so that means he's now $136.5 million richer. I have almost no stock, and this means I am a loser.

News update: Michael is now out of his office. It's as if he never had his geek episode. He slept there throughout the whole day (not unusual at Microsoft), using his *Jurassic Park* inflatable T-Rex toy as a pillow. When he woke up in the early evening, he thanked me for bringing him the Kraft products, and now he says he won't eat anything that's not entirely two-dimensional. 'Ich bin ein Flatlander,' he piped, as he cheerfully sifted through hard copy of the bug-checked code he'd been chugging out. Karla made disgusted clicking noises with her tongue from her office. I think maybe she's in love with Michael.

More details about our group house – Our House of Wayward Mobility.

Because the house receives almost no sun, moss and algae tend to colonize what surfaces they can. There is a cherry tree crippled by a fungus. The rear verandah, built of untreated 2×4's, has quietly rotted away, and the sliding door in the kitchen has been braced shut with a hockey stick to prevent the unwary from straying into the suburban abyss.

The driveway contains six cars: Todd's cherry-red Supra (his life, what little there is of it), my pumpkin Hornet, and four personality-free gray Microsoftmobiles – a Lexus, an Acura Legend, and two Tauri (nerd plural for Taurus). I bet if Bill drove a Shriner's go-cart to work, everybody else would, too.

Inside, each of us has a bedroom. Because of the

Douglas Coupland

McDonald's-like turnover in the house, the public rooms – the living room, kitchen, dining room, and basement – are bleak, to say the least. The dormlike atmosphere precludes heavy-duty interior design ideas. In the living room are two velveteen sofas that were too big and too ugly for some long-gone tenants to take with them. Littered about the Tiki green shag carpet are:

- Two Microsoft Works PC inflatable beach cushions
- One Mitsubishi 27-inch color TV
- Various vitamin bottles
- Several weight-gaining system cartons (mine)
- 86 copies of *MacWEEK* arranged in chronological order by Bug Barbecue, who will go berserk if you so much as move one issue out of date
- Six Microsoft Project 2.0 juggling bean bags
- Bone-shaped chew toys for when Mishka visits
- Two PowerBooks
- Three IKEA mugs encrusted with last month's blender drink sensation
- Two 12.5-pound dumbbells (Susan's)
- A Windows NT box
- Three baseball caps (two Mariners, one A's)
- Abe's Battlestar Galactica trading card album
- Todd's pile of books on how to change your life to win! (*Getting Past OK, 7 Habits of Highly Effective People* . . .)

The kitchen is stocked with ramshackle 1970s avocado green appliances. You can almost hear the ghost of Emily Hartley yelling 'Hi, Bob!' every time you open the fridge door (a sea of magnets and 4-×-6-inch photos of last year's house parties).

Our mail is in little piles by the front door: bills, Star Trek junk mail, and the heap-o-catalogues next to the phone.

I think we'd order our lives via 1–800 numbers if we could.

★　★　★

Mom phoned from Palo Alto. This is the time of year she calls a lot. She calls because she wants to speak about Jed, but none of us in the family are able. We kind of erased him.

I used to have a younger brother named Jed. He drowned in a boating accident in the Strait of Juan de Fuca when I was 14 and he was 12. A Labor Day statistic.

To this day, anything Labor Day-ish creeps me out: the smell of barbecuing salmon, life preservers, Interstate traffic reports from the local radio Traffic Copter, Monday holidays. But here's a secret: My e-mail password is *hellojed*. So I think about him every day. He was way better with computers than I was. He was way nerdier than me.

As it turned out, Mom had good news today. Dad has a big meeting Monday with his company. Mom and Dad figure it's a promotion because Dad's IBM division has been doing so well (by IBM standards – it's not hemorrhaging money). She says she'll keep me posted.

Susan taped laser-printed notes on all of our bedroom doors reminding us about the vesting party this Thursday ('Vest Fest '93'), which was a subliminal hint to us to clean up the place. Most of us work in Building Seven; shipping hell has brought a severe breakdown in cleanup codes.

Susan is 26 and works in Mac Applications. If Susan were a *Jeopardy!* contestant, her dream board would be:

- 680X0 assembly language
- Cats
- Early '80s haircut bands
- 'My secret affair with Rob in the Excel Group'
- Licence plate slogans of America

Douglas Coupland

- Plot lines from *The Monkees*
- The death of IBM

Susan's an IBM brat and hates that company with a passion. She credits it with ruining her youth by transferring her family eight times before she graduated from high school – and the punchline is that the company gave her father the boot last year during a wave of restructuring. So nothing too evil can happen to IBM in her eyes. Her graphic designer friend made up T-shirts saying 'IBM: Weak as a Kitten, Dumb as a Sack of Hammers.' We all wear them. I gave one to Dad last Christmas but his reaction didn't score too high on the chuckle-o-meter. (I am not an IBM brat – Dad was teaching at the University of Western Washington until the siren of industry lured him to Palo Alto in 1985. It was very '80s.)

Susan's a real coding machine. But her abilities are totally wasted reworking old code for something like the Norwegian Macintosh version of Word 5.8. Susan's work ethic best sums up the ethic of most of the people I've met who work at Microsoft. If I recall her philosophy from the conversation she had with her younger sister two weekends ago, it goes something like this:

'It's never been, "We're doing this for the good of society." It's always been us taking an intellectual pride in putting out a good product – and making money. If putting a computer on every desktop and in every home didn't make money, we wouldn't do it.'

That sums up most of the Microsoft people I know.

Microsoft, like any office, is a status theme park. Here's a quick rundown:

- Profitable projects are galactically higher in status than loser (not quite as profitable) projects.
- Microsoft at Work (Digital Office) is sexiest at the moment.

Fortune 500 companies are drooling over DO because it'll allow them to downsize millions of employees. Basically, DO allows you to operate your fax, phone, copier – all of your office stuff – from your PC.

- Cash cows like Word are profitable but not really considered cutting edge.
- Working on-Campus is higher status than being relegated to one of the off-Campus Siberias.
- Having Pentium-driven hardware (built to the hilt) in your office is higher status than having 486 droneware.
- Having technical knowledge is way up there.
- Being an architect is also way up there.
- Having Bill-o-centric contacts is way, way up there.
- Shipping your product on time is maybe the coolest (insert wave of anxiety here). If you ship on time you get a Ship-It award: a 12-×-15-×-1-inch Lucite slab – but you have to pretend it's no big deal. Michael has a Ship-It award and we've tried various times to destroy it – blowtorching, throwing it off the verandah, dowsing it with acetone to dissolve it – nothing works. It's so permanent, it's frightening.

More roommate profiles:

First, Abe. If Abe were a *Jeopardy!* contestant, his seven dream categories would be:

- Intel assembly language
- Bulk shopping
- C++
- Introversion
- 'I love my aquarium'
- How to have millions of dollars and not let it affect your life in any way
- Unclean laundry

Douglas Coupland

Abe is sort of like the household Monopoly-game banker. He collects our monthly checks for the landlord, $235 apiece. The man has millions and he rents! He's been at the group house since 1984, when he was hired fresh out of MIT. (The rest of us have been here, on average, about eight months apiece.) After ten years of writing code, Abe so far shows no signs of getting a life. He seems happy to be reaching the age of 30 in just four months with nothing to his name but a variety of neat-o consumer electronics and boxes of Costco products purchased in rash moments of Costco-scale madness ('Ten thousand straws! Just think of it – only $10 and I'll never need to buy straws ever again!') These products line the walls of his room, giving it the feel of an air-raid shelter.

Bonus detail: There are dried-out patches of sneeze spray all over Abe's monitors. You'd think he could afford 24 bottles of Windex.

Next, Todd. Todd's seven *Jeopardy!* categories would be:

- Your body is your temple
- Baseball hats
- Meals made from combinations of Costco products
- Psychotically religious parents
- Frequent and empty sex
- SEGA Genesis gaming addiction
- The Supra

Todd works as a tester with me. He's really young – 22 – the way Microsoft employees all used to be. His interest is entirely in girls, bug testing, his Supra, and his body, which he buffs religiously at the Pro Club gym and feeds with peanut butter quesadillas, bananas, and protein drinks.

Todd is historically empty. He neither knows nor cares about the past. He reads *Car and Driver* and fields three phone calls a week from his parents who believe that computers are 'the Devil's voice box,' and who try to persuade him to return home to Port Angeles and speak with the youth pastor.

Todd's the most fun of all the house members because he is all impulse and no consideration. He's also the only roomie to have clean laundry consistently. In a crunch you can always borrow an unsoiled shirt from Todd.

Bug Barbecue's seven *Jeopardy!* categories would be:

- Bitterness
- Xerox PARC nostalgia
- Macintosh products
- More bitterness
- Psychotic loser friends
- Jazz
- Still more bitterness

Bug Barbecue is the World's Most Bitter Man. He is (as his name implies) a tester with me at Building Seven. His have-a-life factor is pretty near zero. He has the smallest, darkest room in the house, in which he maintains two small shrines: one to his Sinclair ZX-81, his first computer, and the other to supermodel Elle MacPherson. Man, she'd freak if she saw the hundreds of little photos – the coins, the candles, the little notes.

Bug is 31, and he lets everyone know it. If we ever ask him so much as 'Hey, Bug – have you seen volume 7 of my *Inside Mac*?' he gives a sneer and replies, 'You're obviously of the generation that never built their own motherboard or had to invent their own language.'

Hey, Bug – we love you, too.

Bug never gets offered stock by the company. When payday comes and the little white stock option envelopes with red printing reading 'Personal and Confidential' end up in all of

46   Douglas Coupland

our pigeonholes, Bug's is always, alas, empty. Maybe they're trying to get rid of him, but it's almost impossible to fire someone at Microsoft. It must drive the administration nuts. They hired 3,100 people in 1992 alone, and you know not all of them were gems.

Oddly, Bug is fanatical in his devotion to Microsoft. It's as if the more they ignore him, the more rabidly he defends their honor. And if you cherish your own personal time, you will not get into a discussion with him over the famous Look-&-Feel lawsuit or any of the FTC or Department of Justice actions:

'These litigious pricks piss me off. I wish they'd compete in the marketplace where it really counts instead of being little wusses and whining for government assistance to compete . . .'

You've been warned.

Finally, Michael. Michael's seven *Jeopardy!* categories would be:

- FORTRAN
- Pascal
- Ada (defense contracting code)
- LISP
- Neil Peart (drummer for Rush)
- Hugo and Nebula award winners
- Sir Lancelot

Michael is probably the closest I'll ever come to knowing someone who lives in a mystical state. He lives to assemble elegant streams of code instructions. He's like Mozart to everyone else's Salieri – he enters people's offices where lines of code are written on the dry-erase whiteboards and quietly optimizes the code as he speaks to them, as though someone had written wrong instructions on how to get to the beach and he was merely setting them right so they wouldn't get lost.

He often uses low-tech solutions to high-tech problems: Popsicle sticks, rubber bands, and little strips of paper that turn on a bent coat hanger frame help him solve complex matrix problems. When he moved offices into his new window office (good coder, good office), he had to put Post-it notes reading 'Not Art' on his devices so that the movers didn't stick them under the glass display cases out in the central atrium area.

James Crumley

Bordersnakes

'Crumley writes like an angel on speed . . . Indispensable.'
Time Out

James Crumley's private-eye novels featuring Milo Milodragovitch
and C.W. Sughrue are regarded as masterpieces of contemporary crime
fiction. For the first time in *Bordersnakes* the author who reinvented
the hard-boiled novel unites his two great characters, teaming them
on a journey that fishtails through clouds of dust and pools of blood
from Montana to a cocaine-dusted death trap near the Mexican border.

_____

James Crumley was born in Three Rivers, Texas, and spent most of
his childhood in South Texas. He served three years in the US army
before teaching English as a visiting writer at the University of Texas
at El Paso. *Bordersnakes* is his sixth novel.

Bordersnakes
Available now from Flamingo
ISBN 0 00 655079 7

As we climbed out of the plane the automatic runway landing lights snapped off, leaving us in the soft desert darkness surrounding the small field.

'Castillo, Texas,' the pilot muttered, nervous, removing the dark glasses he always wore for night flying. 'Who the fuck lives out here?'

'*Mojados* – that's wetbacks to you gringos – three kinds of drug smugglers, six different breeds of law dogs, and every kind of criminal ever dreamed up,' the guide answered grimly.

'And over there?' the pilot said, waving his glasses at the smoky, smudged lights across the Rio Grande.

'Enojada?' the guide said, amazed. 'Bordersnakes, man.'

'Who's that?'

'Shit, man,' he finally said, '*nobody* knows who they are. And nobody with any fucking sense gives a shit.'

From a conversation with C.W. Sughrue

Milo

MAYBE IT WAS the goddamned suit. Tailor-made Italian silk, as light and flimsy as shed snakeskin. Or maybe my whole new clean and shiny wardrobe looked strange under my battered old face. A thin knit shirt under the suit coat, woven leather loafers – without socks, of course – and a soft Borsalino felt fedora that made me look like a Russian Black Sea summer pimp. Not bad, though, I thought. For a pimp.

But obviously I had violated more than the dress code in this run-down shithole called Duster's Lounge, a code that surely included a rap sheet at least two pages long, five years' hard time, and all the runny, jailhouse tattoos a man's skin could carry.

Or perhaps the 'roid monkey leaning beside me on the battered bar fancied himself a fashion critic. He sported winged dragons and skulls on the bulging arms hanging out of his muscle shirt, an oversized switchblade in his right hand, and the slobbery leer of a true critic. Whatever, he played with my left cuff until the switchblade pressed into the soft fabric. For the third time in the last two minutes.

'What the fuck you doing here, old man?' he muttered in a downer-freak's growl. 'What the fuck?'

I hadn't even had a sip of my beer yet, my first beer in almost ten years. I tried to turn away peacefully again, smiling tensely without speaking, but the big jerk recaptured my cuff with the point of his knife. Goddamned Sughrue. He'd love this shit.

But he wasn't here. As far as I knew, he could be dead. *But what the hell*, I heard him think, *nobody lives forever*. Gently, I slipped my cuff free.

'Kid, you touch my suit with that blade again,' I said calmly, 'I'm going to shove it up your ass and break it off.' Maybe he'd think it was a joke.

At least he laughed. His voice broke like an adolescent's when he brayed. He honked so loud and long that the steroid acne across his shoulders threatened to erupt. Somewhere in the dim bar, this kid had an audience.

I checked a group of glassy-eyed young men of several races, sporting bloody new tattoos on their arms and military haircuts, who had surrounded two pitchers of thin, bitter beer and one professional woman old enough to be their grandmother. Fort Bliss, I guessed, and the first payday pass of basic training. A half-dozen Sneaky Pete day-drinkers occupied a couple of other tables in the decrepit joint at the desert end of Dyer Street. No problem there. Then I saw the big kid's audience at the shadowed edge of the dance floor: two beefy guys showing lots of ink who could have been tired electricians, unemployed roughnecks, or ex-cons. I addressed them politely.

'Excuse me, gentlemen,' I said loudly, 'perhaps this *vermin* belongs to you?'

The beefy guys made a mock glance over their broad shoulders, then turned wide gap-toothed grins at me. Several daydrinkers chugged their beers and slithered out like greasy shadows. The bartender sidled into the cooler. Then the biggest hunk of beef stood up, laughed, and hitched up his greasy jeans.

'Truth is, sir, Tommy Ray, there,' he said, still grinning, 'he don't much belong to nobody. Seems like the best part of the kid ran down his momma's leg.' Then he paused and glanced at his pal. 'Unfortunately, that'd be my momma, too.'

'Sorry to hear that,' I said, then turned back to the bar to reconsider my new life and wardrobe. And other pressing matters. Such as: why had I brought my ancient bones and new wardrobe into this particular bar on this particular October day in El Paso, Texas? Ten years without so much as a beer, and there I was about to die before I even had a sip of the Coors longneck sweating in front of me.

So I took off my new hat and reached for the beer. Tommy Ray giggled like a fool and missed my cuff this time when he tried to pin it to the scarred bar with the blade, saying, 'What was it you were going to do, old man?' Then he raised a double tequila with the other hand, chugged it, and tossed down a small draft beer to douse the flames.

While he had his head tilted back far enough to stretch his thick neck, I slapped him across the face with the hat and hit him in the windpipe as hard as I could with my right fist. Which should have been hard enough. I'd come into my middle fifties sober and solid. I ran, I pumped iron, and worked the bags, heavy and speed, three times a week. I was still six-foot and two-twenty, with a rock-hard Milodragovitch head. But this kid, like many kids these days, was a monster. Maybe only six-three but a solid two-eighty, with a chin like a middle-buster plow. Even bigger than his big brother. And he stood between me and the sunlight. Grinning.

I cut an eyebrow with a jab, hoping to blind him, then wrapped my right fist in the soft hat and hit him in the face with three straight rights that didn't faze him, didn't even make him stop smiling.

Then I hooked him in the gut. Big mistake. My wrist bent and nearly dislocated. So I grabbed the beer bottle and smashed it against the slimy brass footrail. My first beer in years spattered across the dry wood floor and deeply stained my beautiful new loafers. Maybe the beer would cover the blood. Sure as hell. I'd have to cut this kid just to get out the door; and as much as he deserved to be taken out of the gene pool, I didn't want to be the one to do it. About the time I stopped drinking, I also decided that I'd seen too much death in my life, much too close.

Tommy Ray stepped back into a crouch, his close-set eyes bunched so tightly I might have poked them out with one finger. But his eyelids were probably iron-hard, too. He waved the blade in front of his belt, then rushed me, clubbing at my head with his left and trying for an underhanded sweep with the right. But I caught his left on my shoulder and blocked his sweeping arm with my forearm, a pair of shocks I felt all the way to the bone, then I rolled out, raking the broken bottle across his chest.

Tommy Ray stopped long enough to look down and find his right pectoral, complete with the strap of his muscle shirt and his nipple, flapping off his chest. Then a sheet of blood flowed across his ribs.

In his dazed pause, I meant to drive the beer bottle into his face, then run, but his big brother stepped between us, and the pal pinned me from behind, wrapped me almost gently in his arms. 'Easy, old man,' was all he said.

'Goddammit, TR' the brother said, taking the knife from him, 'you fucking asshole.' Then he turned to me, grabbed my wrist with one hand, and jerked the beer bottle out of it with the other. 'Ah, shit, man, I'm sorry. The fuckin' kid's got the IQ of a spit-warm beer. But he's my little brother. He's just funnin' you . . .'

'Gut strokes are not funny, buddy,' I said.

'I can see how you might feel that way,' he said sincerely, 'and I really am sorry. I should've stopped this shit before somebody got hurt . . .'

'Hurt?' the kid growled as he tried to press the flap of flesh back to his chest. 'The son of a bitch cut my fucking tit off, Rock!'

'You ain't hurt,' his brother said, laughing calmly. 'We'll just sew the fucker back on. Good as new . . .'

Which was the last thing I heard. Tommy Ray slipped to the side and launched a long, slow, looping right hand over his brother's broad shoulder. The fist looked as large as my head and it crunched into the side of my face with a sound like a melon thrown off a speeding truck. I sure as hell wished I had found C. W. Sughrue before I decided to fall off the wagon in this particular wreck.

When I came back to some semblance of consciousness, I found myself still facing afternoon. Late afternoon. The same day, I dearly hoped. The shadows of the rough, prickly mountains that split El Paso like a primitive, sacrificial dagger had only reached the hard-packed parking spaces in front of Duster's.

At least I was in my car, my new Caddy beast, and I had the steering wheel to help me sit upright. As I did, my loafers and hat fell off my chest.

'Jesus,' I muttered, 'fucking kid musta knocked me outa my shoes.'

'True enough, man,' came a voice from beside me. 'And he got Dancer, too, with the back of your head. Dropped him like a cold dog turd. Then I had to hit TR about nine times before he went to one knee.' Big brother held up his right hand. The two middle knuckles were jammed halfway to his wrist, a long deep tooth-cut split the knuckle of his index finger, and his other fingers splayed brokenly from the crooked hand. 'Fuckin' kid always could take a punch.'

'Where's he now?' I asked. When I turned to look around, the wobblies resumed residence in my head, so I had to close my eye. The right one. Tommy Ray had sealed the left one for me. Perhaps forever.

'Police took him to the hospital,' he said. 'Maybe they'll hold him for a while. And with any luck his probation officer will violate him for being drunk. So we're safe for now.' Then he laughed wildly.

'Police?' I said. 'How long have I been out?'

'A good bit,' he said. 'One of my brothers took the call, wrote it up as a wash, but he left me to keep an eye on you. In case you died. Or something.'

'Your brother?'

'Big family, the Soameses, seven brothers,' he said. 'Half cops, half crooks, half crazy.'

'How do you get half of seven?'

'I guess your head's all right, man, you ask a question like that,' he said. 'Sammy Ray drowned in Grenada.'

'How's my eye look?'

'Hamburger,' he said, 'rotten hamburger. Or maybe bloody dog shit. Nothin' a couple of stitches can't fix.'

'Thanks,' I said, 'but I meant the eyeball.'

'Me, too,' he said, then giggled drunkenly. 'It's ugly, but it's okay. And the socket's intact. That's the important part. You've probably got a concussion like a barrel cactus. But the eye will be okay. My old man used to box a little. A ranked heavy for a few minutes, before the booze got him. I worked his corner some when I was a kid.'

'Thanks,' I said, and extended my hand. 'Milodragovitch.'

He waved his bag of bones at me and said, 'Rocky Soames. Rocky Ray. It's a family tradition.'

'Lost fistfights and suicides,' I said, 'that's my family's tradition.'

'Nothin' you could do about it, man. When TR gets behind a handful of downers, somebody has to get hurt,' he said, then grinned. 'Usually several somebodies.'

'Well, fuck it. Next time I decide to have a beer I'll bring a hand grenade,' I said. I would have grinned back at him but it hurt too much.

★ ★ ★

Rocky drove me back to the Paso del Norte Hotel and kindly helped me to my suite. We drew some odd looks as we crossed the lobby, but I crossed some palms, and the looks disappeared. We had plenty of help the rest of the way. After that it was all gravy. A house doctor brought codeine and a half-circle of stitches for the corner of my eye. The bellman took my bloody suit off to the cleaners, then fetched coffee for me, a large glass of tequila for my new buddy, and an extra television set to roll beside my king-sized bed so I could see it with my single working eye.

'Thanks again,' I said to Rocky as he took his leave. 'And tell your little brother that I ain't ever been hit that hard in my whole fucking awful life.'

'Shit, man,' he said, 'everybody tells him that.'

I had to laugh. Maybe it was the drugs. A little later, codeine smooth and towelled warm from a hot tub, I slipped naked between cold expensive sheets. I thought about ordering a scotch the size of West Texas, then knew I shouldn't drink it without Sughrue, and wondered where the fuck he had hidden from me. And why.

When I finally found him three weeks later outside a rock-house convenience store in the tiny West Texas town of Fairbairn, we had both changed so much we didn't even recognize each other. But at least I'd found his hiding place.

Earlier that afternoon, five hours on the interstate east of El Paso, I decided to take the scenic route and turned south on a narrow paved strip that wound through the dry, scrub-brush foothills of the Davis Mountains. In spite of the barbed-wire fences flanking the pavement, I couldn't imagine soft-footed steers grazing across the thin grass scattered among sharp rocks. Maybe sheep or goats. But the rusty, four-string barbed-wire fence couldn't hold a goat. Or even the world's dumbest walking mutton.

After thirty minutes on the little highway without seeing a soul – not even a buzzard – I spotted a small herd of longhorns among a patch of thorned brush hopelessly trying to crawl up the genetic ladder toward treedom. When I stopped to stare at the cattle, they stared back, their wild eyes perfectly at home in that reckless landscape, their gaze as rank and rangy as the African breed that began their bloodline. I wondered how the hell those drovers managed to herd these beasts from West Texas to Montana in the 1880s without Cobra gunships.

Then I began to see people: a welder hanging the blade back on a grader that had been scratching a firebreak out of the stony scrub; two Mexican hands greasing a windmill under a sky swept pale, polished blue by the constant wind; an old woman in a tiny Ford Escort running her RFD route, bringing the mail to the scattered, shotgunned mailboxes along the road.

At a Y intersection with an even smaller highway, I had to stop to let a funeral cortege pass, though I couldn't imagine a graveyard in the middle of this nowhere. The next vehicle I met was a pickup that contained three teenage boys with faces painted like clowns under their broad cowboy hats. I don't know what I'd expected in West Texas, but I began to suspect that I had wandered into a fucking Fellini film.

Then came the tourists as I climbed past slopes of juniper and scrub oak, and higher still into the improbable grey rock peaks: a busload of ancients turning into a picnic ground already occupied by several families in vans; a couple of drug-store cowboys drinking beer at a turnout; and a group of hikers who looked like retired college professors. Then I saw the MacDonald Observatory rising from the mountain ridge like an escaping moon.

Too weird, I thought, too fucking weird. So I stopped at the next wide spot in the road to collect myself, wondering what I'd done, wondering what the hell I was doing in West Texas.

James Crumley

Tim Dorsey

Florida Roadkill

'I loved this. Thomas Pynchon hacks it out with Hunter S.
Thompson: referee, Elmore Leonard. But much more, too. I
was close to being sick with laughter at times, other times just
close to being sick. Great fun.'

M. JOHN HARRISON, author of *Signs of Life*

As Sean Breen and David Klein head out from Tampa Bay on their
long-planned trip to the Florida Keys there's nothing on their minds
except fishing, beer and baseball. But when five million dollars is
dropped into the boot of the wrong car, a whole convoy of homicidal
wackos sets off in pursuit of the two unsuspecting men, leaving behind
a bewildering trail of bodies.

From murder by shrink-fit jeans in Tampa, via mayhem at the World
Series in Miami, to a convention of Hemingway lookalikes in Key
West, *Florida Roadkill* is an unforgettable ride through the wildest
corners of the Sunshine State – a kaleidoscopic crime spree taking in
sex, drugs and Satanist rock 'n' roll, lap dancing, extortion and a dozen
of the most unusual forms of murder ever seen in fiction.

Tim Dorsey is thirty-eight years old and grew up in Riviera Beach
on Florida's south-east coast. For the last five years he has worked as
a journalist on the night desk of the *Tampa Tribune*. As a result, he
regularly has to sort through reports of brutal and strange crimes.
Humour is a natural defence reaction to editing this day-in-day-out
parade of dysfunction, violence and stupidity, and it's led to a sort of
surreal, Florida-noir way of looking at things that became his extraordinary first novel, *Florida Roadkill* – a hyper, jump-cut, manic black
comedy and high-voltage crime tale. He is currently working on a
second novel, due to be published by HarperCollins in 2000.

Florida Roadkill
Available now from HarperCollins
ISBN 0 00 651305 0

CLINTON ELLROD PAINTED white block letters in an arc across the front window of the Rapid Response convenience store. Back behind the cash register, he admired his handiwork through the glass, reading in reverse: 'Congratulations Marlins!'

With the efficiency of a casino worker, Ellrod pulled down two packs of Doral menthols, tore loose five scratch-off lottery tickets (the sand dollars game), rang up a twelve-pack of ice-brewed beer and set pump seven for eighteen dollars.

Ellrod, like all Florida convenience store clerks, had the Serengeti alertness of the tastiest gazelle in the herd. He studied customers for danger. He ruled out the pair at the chips rack, the tall, athletic guy and the shorter, bookish man exchanging playful punches, debating Cheetos, puffy or crunchy.

Ellrod made change for a bookie on Rollerblades. A black Mercedes S420 limousine pulled up. Three Latin men slammed three doors. They wore identical white linen suits, shirts open at the collar, no chest hair or gold chains. Thick, trimmed moustaches. They entered the store in descending order of height and in the same order filled three Styrofoam cups at the soda spigot.

The athletic guy used a twenty to pay for two bags of Cheetos and a tank of regular unleaded; they drove to the edge of the convenience store lot in a white Chrysler and waited for the stoplight at the corner to hold up traffic, then rejoined US 1 southbound.

The tallest Latin asked Ellrod for the *servicio*, and Ellrod pointed to the rear of the store. All three went inside the one-toilet restroom and closed the door. Ellrod turned to the beeping gas control panel. He pressed a button and leaned to a grape-size microphone on a gooseneck. 'Pump number four is on.'

'About fucking time,' said the speaker on the control panel. The pickup truck at pump four sat on tractor tires. It was red, spangled metallic, with a bank of eight amber fog lights over the cab. The sticker on the left side of the bumper read, 'English only in the USA!' The one on the right had a drawing of the Stars and Stripes. It said, 'Will the last American out of Miami please bring the flag?'

The driver walked into the store, and Ellrod saw he came to five-nine on the robber height guide running up the doorjamb. He had a crew cut midway between Sid Vicious and H. R. Haldeman, a Vandyke beard and a sunburnt face rounded out into a moon by the people at Pabst Blue Ribbon. He wore the official NFL jersey of the Dallas Cowboys.

'What took you so long, stupid!' said the driver.

'That'll be nineteen dollars,' Ellrod said without interest. The man pulled bills from his wallet; his face had a dense patina of perspiration. Ellrod smelled whiskey, onions and BO.

'I asked you a question!' said the driver. He looked up from his wallet and saw Ellrod's T-shirt. 'FIU? What the fuck's that? Some new shitty rap band?!'

Ellrod, African-American, picked up the drift of the conversation.

'Florida International University,' he said evenly.

'Oh, you and the homeboys now stealing college laundry.'

'I go to school there.'

'Don't bullshit me, boy. You're so smart, how come you workin' *here*?' The man pointed to the employee parking space and Ellrod's two-hundred-thousand-mile Datsun with a trash bag for a back window. 'That's your car, isn't it! Shit, don't go telling me you're a college boy. I didn't even graduate high school and look at my truck!'

Ellrod glanced out at pump number four and the rolling monument to pinheads everywhere. The store audio system piped in 'Right Place, Wrong Time' and it was to the part about 'refried confusion'.

'Now give me my fucking change, you stupid fucking . . .'

And he said it. The word. It hung in the air between them, an electrical cumulonimbus over the cash register.

The driver realized what he'd spoken and paused to flash back. He used the word once to criticise a bad parking job at a Wendy's, and this little four-foot guy went Tasmanian Devil on him. He received bruised ribs, a jaw wired shut and eight fog lights snapped off his truck.

He panicked. He jumped back from the counter and pulled a switchblade on Ellrod. 'Don't try anything! You know you guys call each other that all the time! Don't go getting on me about slavery!'

The tallest Latin was next in line, fiddling with a point-of-purchase display, key-chain flashlights in the shape of AK-47 bullets.

'Hey!' the Latin said to the pickup driver. 'Apologize!'

The driver turned the blade toward him. 'Fuck off, Julio! You don't even have a dog in this fight! Go back to your guacamole farm and those tropical monkeys you call the mothers of your children!'

The driver never saw it. A second Latin came from behind, holding a bottle of honey-mustard barbecue sauce the size of a bowling pin. He had it by the neck and swung it around into the driver's nose, which exploded. Blood squirted everywhere like someone had stomped the heel of a boot down on a packet of ketchup.

Ellrod witnessed an entirely new league of violence. Everything in his experience up to now, even murder, was amateur softball. The driver was swarmed as he fell, and the Latins came up with makeshift convenience store weapons. Dry cell battery, meat tenderizer, Parrot Gardens car deodorizer. In ten seconds, they pulverized both elbows, both kneecaps and both testicles.

The tallest Latin walked to the rotisserie next to the soda machine. A dozen hot dogs had turned on a circle of spits for six hours, and they were leathery and resistant to conventional forks and knives. He grabbed two of the spits and held one in each fist, pointing down, like daggers. The others saw him and cleared away from the pickup driver, now on his back. The tall one pounced and drove the spits into the driver's chest, a bull-fight *banderillero* setting the decorative spears. One spit pierced the right lung, and the other blew a ventricle. The driver torqued and shimmied on the floor and then fell into the death rattle, two shrivelled-up hot dogs quivering on rabbit-ear antennas sticking out of his chest.

The tall Latin stepped over the driver and up to the cash register. He pulled a ten from an eelskin wallet and handed it to Ellrod. 'Three Cokes and two Jumbo Meaty Dogs.'

Ellrod's legs vibrated under the counter, but he managed to make change. After a half minute, he ran to the window and watched the limousine merge into southbound traffic on US 1. The windows were down and he could see three men sucking soda straws.

Sean Breen ran his finger down the triple-A map on his lap, a steady flow of crunchy Cheetos going to his mouth with the free hand. In the driver's seat, David Klein had a thing going with a bag of the puffies.

Fifteen miles south of Miami. Sean said, 'Cutler Ridge.' He

Tim Dorsey

looked up from the map and out the window. 'Can hardly tell Hurricane Andrew came through. You should have been here five years ago. That business tower there. You could see in all the offices. The east face was gone.'

Twelve more miles they hit Florida City. The Turnpike came in from the northeast and dumped onto US 1. The end of civilization on the mainland. The peninsula had twenty more miles until the bridge to the Florida Keys, but the only thing left was a two-lane road south through the mangroves. The final building before the wilderness, the Last Chance Saloon, had a 'Go Marlins!' banner over the door between the wagon wheels.

Sean and David thought professional wrestling in Florida wasn't what it used to be.

'Jack Brisco was my favourite,' said Sean. 'His trademark was the Figure-Four Leg-Lock.'

'Those were the days, when the fundamentals meant something.'

'Like the sleeper hold.'

'Remember you had to apply an antidote hold after the sleeper knocked the guy unconscious?'

'Yeah, and one time this masked wrestler wouldn't let anyone in the ring to apply the antidote to his opponent, and Gordon Solie was going crazy in the announcer's booth, yelling, "Brain damage is setting in!" The guy went into a coma and came out of it the following week to win the battle royal.'

David's face turned serious. Ahead, a dark lump sat in the lane. David winced as it passed under the car, and relaxed when it cleared the undercarriage.

He looked in the rearview. 'Gopher tortoise,' he said. 'Ain't gonna make it.'

David pulled over and walked back toward the tortoise, which had reached the centre line. He stood on the shoulder, waiting for opportunity. Heavy traffic blowing by, but a break coming up. One more car to go and he could run out and carry the tortoise to the other side.

Serge leaned forward in the passenger seat and tuned the radio in the canary-yellow '72 Corvette. His yellow beach shirt matched the car and was covered with palm trees; his two-dollar sunglasses had ruby frames and alligators at the corners. The first four radio stations were Spanish, then blues from Miami, then Serge found the frequency he wanted as they passed the Last Chance Saloon.

'*I just want to celebrate . . . another day of living . . .*'

Serge talked over the radio. 'And what was the deal with Coral Key State Park? The place was a death-trap. If it wasn't for Flipper, someone would have died there every week. Can't believe nobody sued.'

'Dolphins like to wear hats,' said Coleman, a joint dangling from his lips as he drove. On his head was one of those afro wigs painted in a rainbow. He was wearing novelty sunglasses with slinky eyeballs, and they swung and clacked together when he turned to face Serge.

'*. . . I just want to celebrate . . . yeah! yeah! . . .*'

'What's that in the road?' asked Serge.

'Don't know,' said Coleman. 'Looks like something fell out of a car and that guy's trying to retrieve it. Some kind of case . . . Well not today, fella!'

Coleman swerved over the centre line, like Jerry Lewis running over Spencer Tracy's hat in *It's a Mad, Mad, Mad, Mad World.*

'*. . . I just want to celebrate another day of living! . . .*'

And Coleman popped the turtle.

The pair turned around and saw a guy jumping up and down in the road, shaking his fists in the air.

'You sick fuck! Why'd you do that?!' Serge shouted. 'You killed a living thing!'

'I thought it was a helmet,' Coleman said.

'A helmet? We're in the Keys! This ain't fuckin' *Rat Patrol*!'

Serge plucked the joint from Coleman's lips – 'Gimme that!' – and flicked it out the window. He ripped the slinky-eyeball glasses off Coleman's face and tossed them in the open gym bag at his feet. The glasses landed on the packs of hundred-dollar bills and next to the Smith & Wesson .38.

'Pull over,' said Serge. 'I'm driving.'

Twenty miles west of Key West, mangrove islets scattered across jade shallows. Toward the Gulf Stream, the green gave way at once to a cold, ultramarine blue that ran to the horizon. It was noon, a soundless, cloudless day, and the sun broiled.

At the far end of the silence began a buzz, like a mosquito. It stayed low for a long time and then suddenly swelled into a high-precision, motorized thunder that prevented any train of thought, and a forty-foot cigarette boat slapped and crashed across the swells far closer to the flats than was smart.

Orange and aqua stripes ran the length of the speedboat, which had the logo of the Miami Dolphins on one side and a big number 13 on the other.

Behind the wheel was twenty-two-year-old Johnny Vegas, bronzed, built and smelling like a whorehouse. Because he was wearing Whorehouse Cologne, one hundred dollars an ounce on South Beach. Long black hair straight back in the wind, herringbone gold chain around his neck. His workout T-shirt had the sleeves cut off and a cartoon on the front that made a joke about his shlong being big. On the back was a drawing of a woman in a bikini with a bull's-eye on her crotch. He wore the curved sunglasses of a downhill skier.

Johnny's mouth alternated between a thousand-candle-power shit-eating grin and running his tongue over his gums with cocaine jitters. He kept the coke in a twenty-four-carat gold shark amulet he'd bought in a head shop on Key West, Southernmost Bong and Hookah. It now hung from the gold chain. He threw two toggles near the ignition and 'Smoke on the Water' shook from sixteen waterproof speakers.

Johnny lived off a trust fund generated by a life-insurance-for-the-elderly program targeting anyone who had ever been, known, seen or heard about a military veteran. He exercised daily in his Bal Harbor condo and it showed – not muscle-bound but defined at six feet, one-ninety. On weekends he cruised for chicks in the boat, and he had the tan of a professional beach volleyball player.

Other people bought jerseys with the numbers of their favourite Miami Dolphins players. Johnny customized the cigarette boat for his favourite, future Hall of Fame quarterback Dan Marino. He soon found that people assumed it actually was Marino's boat, and that Johnny was a tight friend. Johnny often said, yes, it was Marino's boat. Would you like to come aboard, little girl?

In romance, Johnny was a selective man. He wouldn't just go for anyone. He was attracted to a very specific type: horny, young, binge-drinking women in T-backs. Any event with a hint of spring-break attitude, Johnny's boat was there.

He ranged from Fort Lauderdale to Islamorada in the Keys, where fast boats held effective parties on an offshore sandbar. That was as far as Vegas would take the cigarette. The cocaine he bought for the World Series the night before had taken him the rest of the way down the Keys.

No sooner had he arrived, he was on the business side of Key West, heading out to sea. As the propeller cavitated, Johnny unconsciously fingered the coke talisman hanging at his sternum. At sixty miles an hour, he strained to see as the air pressure

68   Tim Dorsey

flattened his eyeballs, but he had to keep up appearances for the woman clinging to her white leather seat. She didn't really mind, with a tight belly full of Captain Morgan.

She was maybe twenty, a student at Key West Community College, majoring in flirting her way onto expensive boats with powder parties. She was thin with a deep tan, sun-lightened brown hair and a cute Georgia face. And she'd learned nothing in life is free when she got thrown overboard by an Argentinean tycoon on whose yacht she had been partying and whose knee she'd been grabbing before she said, 'Sorry, I have a boyfriend back at school.'

That morning Johnny had been idling the boat past Mallory Square when he spotted her sitting in a bikini with legs hanging over the seawall, having shown up ten hours early for the sunset celebration.

He tapped his left nostril; she nodded eagerly and boarded. They did two lines at the docks and slugged rumrunners as they passed Sand Key lighthouse.

Johnny's plan was to head south from Key West, pick up deeper water and chart west. The uninhabited Marquesas Atoll sat twenty-five miles further with a sandy beach, perfect for scoring.

Which would be a first. Because, despite the boat and the exercising and the cocaine and cologne and money, he never got a babe in the sack. Not once. It was always something. Boat fire, water spout, sand crabs, Coast Guard search, language barrier, drug overdose and, with rampant frequency, the sudden and complete change of heart. There was even the can't-miss time a statuesque brunette model came right up to him on the dock and said, 'I fuck guys with fast boats.' They were three miles offshore and she's topless, taking off her bottom, when she hears something. A hydroplane pulls up, a man opens the cockpit, and she gets in and leaves.

This time would be different. This time with – what was her

name? One of those double, singsong deals. Something Sue. Betty Sue? Peggy Sue? Ah, to hell with it: more cocaine for everyone!

Indications to the contrary, Johnny wasn't obnoxious, just immature, and the older residents of his condominium regarded him as a loveable, goofy pet. They also had no faith in his seamanship. They worried that someday he'd hit an awash coral head and there would go Johnny, cartwheeling across the Gulf Stream at eighty miles an hour until he was embedded head-first in the sand like a javelin. So they broke it down for him. Stay in the blue water and out of the green water. Over and over: blue water good, green water bad.

Johnny and 'Sue raced due south of the Marquesas in solid-green water and skirting closer to yellow and white. The water was clear as a swimming pool, and patches of sand and coral ran starboard. Between two islands was a channel that cut across the flats as if someone had poured a river of lime Jell-O. He looked down and saw the shadow of his boat racing next to him on the sea floor, and he pretended he was the Flying Dutchman.

The bottom was soft, and Johnny's boat ploughed a hundred-yard trench that bled off the violence of the grounding. The stop catapulted 'Sue onto the deck on her hands and knees.

'Are we stuck?' she asked, the boat's deck as solid and unmoving as Nebraska.

'Oh, no no no!' said Johnny. He tossed a mushroom anchor over the bow with forty feet of line, which was thirty-nine too many, and the excess coils of rope floated by where 'Sue was sitting.

'How 'bout some more cocaine!' said Johnny, creating a diversion. He tapped the amulet on the fibreglass console. 'Sue poured another rumrunner out of Johnny's titanium tactical party Thermos, having spilled the last one down the left side of her bikini top. Johnny took off his shirt.

The stereo blared 'Funky Cold Medina'. They climbed up on the bow. Dancing sloppy, not holding each other, rubbing chests. Johnny thought of his buzz and 'Sue and the music and how he was gonna finally get laid. He closed his eyes and saw an infomercial for Veterans' Health and Life on the inside of the eyelids, and he smiled.

There was a splash in the water off port, and Johnny and 'Sue tumbled back together on the bow.

'Jesus, Harry and Joseph!' he yelled.

They looked overboard, out in the blue water, where their boat should have been. They expected to see a bale of dope or an aeroplane wing, but instead saw a large blob covered with seaweed and algae and gunk, a long-dead manatee or Kemp's ridley turtle.

They stared a half minute, and their crunched-up faces released at the same time with recognition. Out in the water was a man, bloated and distended, chain around his neck. 'Sue gave a prolonged, blood-clotting scream, which Johnny took to mean she was no longer in the mood.

It took a few minutes but 'Sue had started to calm down, just sniffling and her chest heaving a little. Johnny thought, yeah, there's a blown-up old dead guy all putrid and shit a few feet away, but I got the smooth moves! He put his arm around her shoulder, to console her, and began sliding his hand toward her breast.

A procession of sports cars and RVs was making the grunion run down from Florida City to the drawbridge onto Key Largo. Because of speeding, reckless driving and head-on crashes, the Florida Department of Transportation erected a bunch of warning signs and built special passing lanes.

One of the signs read, 'Be patient. Passing lane one mile.' Next to it, an Isuzu Rodeo towing a Carolina Skiff jack-knifed trying to pass a Ranchero. The Rodeo slid upright to a stop on the left shoulder, but the skiff rolled, sending four cases of Bud and Bud Lite clattering across the road. The rigid column of high-speed traffic became unorganized, like a line of ants hit with bug spray. A Mustang swerved left, flipped and landed half-submerged in the water next to the causeway; a Mercury spun out to the right and slid down the embankment sideways, taking out thirty feet of endangered plants. Motorists ran to check on the people in the Isuzu but retreated when the Mercury's driver pulled a nickel .45 out of the glove compartment. He opened fire on the Rodeo, across the street, which returned fire with an SKS Chinese military rifle. The Rodeo's bumper sticker said, 'Hang up and drive!'

Behind the firefight, people got out of cars crouched behind bumpers or ran for cover in the mangroves. Some jumped in Barnes and Blackwater Sounds and swam away.

Twenty cars back from the accident, Sean Breen and David Klein opened their doors for shields and prepared to run. Ten cars back, three Latin men sat in a bullet-proof Mercedes limousine, playing three Nintendo GameBoys.

One car back was a yellow Corvette. Coleman and Serge stared at the boat in the middle of the road and the foam shooting into the air from the Budweisers.

As they approached Key Largo, breaks in the roadside brush had given first glimpses of the Keys. Hundreds of yards of tangled branches blurring by, and then a two-foot opening, a subliminal view across the sounds. Unnamed mangrove islands in that unmistakable profile, long and low. Serge thought it was the same profile that in 1513 prompted Ponce de Leon's sailors to name them Los Martires, the martyrs, because they looked like dead guys lying down. No they don't, thought Serge, but he was naturally high anyway as he sat in the parked Corvette. The sniper fire was making a racket and it snapped Serge out of it.

'Beer me,' he said, looking straight ahead.

'Right,' said Coleman. He waited a few seconds for a break in the gunfire and ran out in the road in front of the car, grabbing one of the few cans that wasn't blowing suds from the seams.

He jumped back in the car and handed it to Serge.

Serge stared at him. 'I meant from the cooler.'

Eleven months before the World Series, in November, the start of the tourist season, the beaches off St Petersburg were jammed with pasty people.

As always, Sharon Rhodes knew every eye was on her as she walked coyly along the edge of the surf, twirling a bit of hair with a finger. A volleyball game stopped. Footballs and Frisbees fell in the water. Guys lost track of conversations with their wives and got socked.

She was the *Sports Illustrated* swimsuit edition in person. Six feet tall, gently curling blond hair cascading over her shoulders and onto the top of her black bikini. She had a Carnation Milk face with high cheekbones and a light dusting of freckles. Her lips were full, pouty and cruel in the way that makes men drive into buildings.

She stopped as if to think, stuck an index finger in her lips and sucked. Men became woozy. She turned and splashed out into three feet of water and dunked herself. When she came up, she shook her head side to side, flinging wet blond hair, and thrust out her nipples.

There was nothing in Sharon a man wanted to love, caress or defend. This was tie-me-up-and-hurt-me stuff, everything about her shouting at a man, 'I will destroy all that is dear to you,' and the man says, 'yes, please.'

Wilbur Putzenfus was losing hair on top and working the comb-over. No tan. No tone. A warrior of the business cubicle, with women he was socially retarded. Spiro Agnew without the power. A hundred and fifty pounds of unrepentant geek-on-wheels.

Sharon threw her David Lee Roth beach towel down next to his, lay on her stomach and untied her top.

Wilbur studied Sharon with a series of stolen glimpses that wouldn't have been so obvious if they hadn't been made through the viewfinder of a camcorder.

When Wilbur ran out of videotape, Sharon raised up on her elbows, tits hanging, and said to him in a low, husky voice, 'I like to do it in public.'

Wilbur was apoplectic.

Sharon replaced her top and stood up. She reached down, took Wilbur by the hand and tried to get him to his feet, but his legs didn't work right. It was like Bambi's first steps.

She walked him over to the snack bar and showers. Against a thicket of hibiscus was one of those plywood cutouts, the kind with a hole that tourists stick their faces through for snapshots.

This one had a large cartoon shark swallowing a tourist feet first. The tourist wore a straw hat, had a camera hanging from a strap around his neck, and was banging on the shark's snout.

The bushes shielded the backside of the plywood from public view, but the front faced heavy foot traffic on the boardwalk.

Sharon told Wilbur to put his face in the hole and he complied. She told him not to take his head out of the hole or she would permanently stop what she was doing. She pulled his plaid bathing trunks to his ankles, kneeled down and applied her expertise.

Some of the guys from the volleyball game had been following Sharon like puppy dogs and they peeked behind the plywood. Then they walked around the front of the cutout and stood on the sidewalk, pointing and laughing at Wilbur. Word spread.

The crowd was over a hundred by the time Wilbur's saliva

started to meringue around his mouth. His eyes came unplugged and rolled around in their sockets, and he made sounds like Charlie Callas.

Finally, nearing crescendo, Wilbur stared bug-eyed at the crowd and yelled between shallow breaths, 'WILL...YOU...MAR-RY...ME?'

'Yeth,' came the answer from behind the plywood, a female voice with a mouth full, and the crowd cheered.

Magnus Mills

The Restraint of Beasts

'**A demented, deadpan comic wonder**.'   THOMAS PYNCHON

Meet Tam and Richie: two dour Scots labourers. Fond of denim, workshy, permanently discontented, intent on getting to the pub every night come hell or high water – in short, just your average workmen. But Tam and Richie, with their new supervisor, begin to display hidden depths. Despatched to a farmsite in England by their boss Donald, they deal conclusively with first one then another client, all the while sticking unbendingly to their rituals until comeuppance arrives to herd them away. But just who exactly are the Hall Brothers, and what do they farm?

————————

Magnus Mills failed his 11–plus in 1965 and was then placed in the hands of Gloucestershire Education Authority. He later worked with dangerous machinery in Britain and Australia, before obtaining his recent employment as a London bus driver. His first novel, *The Restraint of Beasts*, was shortlisted for both the Booker Prize and the Whitbread First Novel Award, and has already been translated into fifteen different languages.

Flamingo publishes Mills's second novel, *All Quiet on the Orient Express*, in September 1999.

The Restraint of Beasts
Available now from Flamingo
ISBN 0 00 655114 9

MARINA LIVED IN a small flat above a shoe shop.

'Very nice,' I said, as we went in.

'It's only temporary,' she replied.

She was supposed to be making coffee, but somehow we never got round to it. Not long afterwards we entered the bedroom, where I noticed there were two single beds, each with a cabinet covered in women's things.

'Whose is that?' I asked, pointing to the extra bed.

'My flatmate's,' said Marina. 'She's staying at a friend's tonight.'

'That's handy,' I remarked.

'Yes,' she said, 'I suppose it is.'

I looked at her and realized that underneath her clothes she was completely naked. A few minutes later we lay quietly on the bed, and it felt as if I was alone with this girl on a remote and distant planet.

Then I remembered Tam and Richie.

'Not quite alone,' I heard myself say.

'Pardon?' she said.

'Sorry, nothing,' I answered, but the spell was broken. There wasn't much room in the bed and I hardly got any sleep.

In the morning Marina had to go to work and there was no breakfast. As we parted she said, 'I'm not a fence post, you know.'

I wasn't sure what she meant by that.

I went and bought some doughnuts in a cake shop. I had no idea where Tam and Richie could have got to, and wasn't sure what to do. I was reluctant to phone up Donald and tell him I'd lost them. Somehow I expected to see them at any minute, still wandering around the streets, possibly looking for me, but more likely waiting for the pubs to open again. I patrolled the town for a while, but they were nowhere to be seen. In deep thought I drove back to Upper Bowland. I dismissed the idea that Tam and Richie might have found their own way there. They had shown no interest in local geography since their arrival in England, and as far as I knew had hardly any money left. I was therefore surprised to find them both asleep in the caravan, fully clothed, Richie on his bed and Tam on mine. They stirred as I went inside, but I didn't wake them. For some reason I felt slightly indebted to them, and as soon as I saw them lying there asleep I decided to give them the day off.

I made myself some eggs for breakfast and after a while they woke.

'Morning,' I said.

'Do you have to say that every day?' replied Tam.

'What?' I asked.

'Mor-ning,' he said, in a sing-song sort of voice.

'It's fucking sarcastic, isn't it,' added Richie.

'Sorry,' I said.

They didn't seem very grateful when I said they could have the day off. I thought they would appreciate the gesture. I also hoped that they might get bored after a while and get round to cleaning up the mess in the caravan, or even decide to come and do some work on the fence after all. In the event they did none of these things. They just stayed in the caravan all day long, smoking, and waiting for me to come back so we could go out again.

In the meantime I spent the day working on my own, putting a couple of straining posts in the ground, and doing a bit of

Magnus Mills

joinery. Around mid-afternoon I decided to walk over the hill, checking the two cross-fences, measuring them, and making sure we hadn't forgotten to do anything.

It was then that I found we had a visitor. I was just testing the wire tension near the top of the hill when I saw a man coming along the fence from the other end. For a moment I thought Mr Perkins had come to have a look, but I soon realized that this was someone altogether different. I'd only seen Mr Perkins in the darkness, but I knew this wasn't him. The visitor was a very big man in a rustic suit, and reminded me of a large pig. He appeared to be giving the fence a thorough examination as he walked along, tugging on the occasional wire and pushing the posts to see if they moved. When he got to the point where the two fences crossed he stopped. There were no gates up here because there was no need for any. All the gates were to be positioned at points around the foot of the hill, so his way was effectively barred. I registered the exact moment he noticed me as he looked left and then right, but he failed to give any acknowledgement. It was as if I was a mere fixture or fitting. He just carried on studying the details of the fence.

However, my presence was enough to prevent him from attempting to climb over, which I think he would have done if I hadn't been there. Instead, he stayed where he was, and ignored me as I approached. At last I stood directly opposite him at the other side of the fence. Only then did he look at me.

'Keeping busy?' he said.

'Just about,' I replied.

'That's good.' He turned sideways and stared out across the hillside. I waited. Then he looked at the sky.

'Met Perkins?' he asked.

'Only once,' I said.

'Don't talk to me about Perkins.'

In the awkward silence that followed he again began to

examine the fence, frowning with preoccupation and glancing at me from time to time. Finally, he cast his eye along the line of posts.

'Exemplary,' he remarked, and began stalking off down the hill.

'And you're Mr . . . ?' I called after him.

'Hall,' he said over his shoulder. 'John Hall.'

I stood by the fence absorbing this information. At last I had come face to face with one of the Hall Brothers, but I still had no idea why he was so interested in our fence. It struck me that he didn't really look like a fencer at all. He was certainly a heavily built man, but a lot of it was fat. Somehow I just couldn't picture him digging post holes or swinging the post hammer. I wondered what the other brothers were like. Maybe it was them who built the fences and he was the brains behind the organization. Perhaps his brothers were big too, but more solid. Like barn doors. I realized that I was beginning to speculate like Tam, so I put Mr Hall out of my mind and carried on with my work. The weather had dried up, but was beginning to turn cool, and as dusk came a chilly breeze started to blow across the hillside. Finally I made my way back to the caravan.

When I'd gone down for my lunch Tam and Richie had been lolling about on their beds, passing the time doing nothing. Now, however, they sat looking out of the window, evidently awaiting my return. They'd even gone to the trouble of putting the kettle on.

As soon as I went into the caravan Richie said, 'There was a guy snooping round here this afternoon.'

'Was there?' I said, pretending not to be very interested.

'Big, fat fucker,' added Tam.

When I showed no reaction, Richie stood up and pulled a note out of his back pocket. 'He left this for you.'

The note was folded into four. I opened it and read 'See you here at eight o'clock.' It was signed J. Hall.

I glanced at Tam and Richie. They were both staring hard at me. It was obvious they must have read the note, but I said nothing and folded it up again. At last Tam could contain himself no longer. He leapt to his feet and shouted at the top of his voice, 'They're coming to get us!'

In doing so he somehow managed to smash the gas lamp at his end of the caravan, so that bits of glass flew everywhere, including into the waiting teapot.

'Alright, alright,' I said. 'We don't know what they want, do we?'

'Don't be a cunt,' said Richie. 'You know why they're coming.'

Tam stuck his face in mine. 'YAAAAAAAAAAAH!' he cried. 'YAAAAAAAAH!' After he'd calmed down a bit I got him to clear up the glass and I had my tea. Then we began to wait for eight o'clock. I had been planning to go down to the phone box this evening to give Donald a progress report, but decided under the circumstances that it was better to defer the call for the time being. At half past seven I put some water on to have a shave. I didn't see why I should change my arrangements just because someone said they were coming at eight o'clock. As usual Tam and Richie watched the whole process. At ten to eight there was nothing left to do but sit and wait. Eight o'clock finally came and nothing happened. At ten past, however, some headlights swung up the track from the road. All three of us had our boots on, so we stepped out of the caravan into the yard. A moment later a large car appeared and drove up to where we stood.

Mr Hall was already speaking as he opened the door and got out.

'Right,' he announced. 'I want you to do some fencing for me. When can you start?'

In the dim light cast from the caravan I noticed that the rustic suit had gone and he was now wearing a white coat. The sort worn by butchers. It took me a second to register what he had said.

'We can't,' I replied. 'We're already working for a company.'

Mr Hall then did what he had done on the hill in the afternoon, and completely ignored me.

'There's eight hundred yards to do by Monday, so the sooner you start the better,' he said. 'How much gold will you want for doing that?'

He thrust his hands in his coat pocket, looked at the ground and waited. I found myself looking at the ground as well.

'So?' he said.

I glanced up at him, thinking he would still be looking at the ground. Instead his eyes were fixed on me.

'We're working for somebody else,' I said.

At this moment I sensed that Tam wanted to say something, but he and Richie had both slipped into their usual silent routine, so it was all left to me.

'You'll have to do it as a foreigner,' said Mr Hall. 'Come on, we'll go for a drink.' He opened the back door of his car and indicated that the three of us should get in. Then he drove us to the Queen's Head. On the way out we rolled slowly past the new HALL BROS. fence, which he silently scrutinized from behind the wheel, post by post.

As we walked into the pub, the landlord was slouching over the bar reading a newspaper. The moment he saw Mr Hall he practically stood to attention. 'Evening, John,' he boomed. Likewise, several drinkers around the bar greeted Mr Hall by his first name, but in the same subservient way, as if doing so conferred some sort of honour on them. Meanwhile, Tam, Richie and myself were treated as if we were new disciples. One of the locals winked at us and tapped his nose significantly, after first glancing at Mr Hall to make sure he wasn't looking.

'Give these lads a pint apiece and rustle them up some grubbage,' ordered Mr Hall.

Magnus Mills

He turned to us. 'You haven't eaten, have you?'

We had, but we all shook our heads.

He led us over to our usual table in the corner and we sat down. The landlord bustled over with a tray bearing our drinks. Mr Hall, I noticed, was drinking orange squash.

'Everything alright, John?' said the landlord. I was surprised he didn't say Sir, or even King, John.

John Hall ignored him and sipped his squash. 'Bloody stuff,' he said.

The landlord retreated, and then there was an expectant silence, which I finally broke. 'Is that a butcher's coat?' I said.

'Yes it is,' he replied. 'We're butchers. Should have stayed that way as well.'

We nodded but said nothing, and he went on.

'Started as butchers and then we bought some land and raised our own beasts. Then we had too many beasts and had to buy more land and replace the fences. That's how we got into fencing, but we've taken on too much work.'

'Who does the fencing?' I asked.

'My brother,' he replied.

'What, on his own?'

Tam and Richie, who had been silently studying their pints, both looked up at Mr Hall.

'Course not,' he said. 'Got some lads in to do it, but they've gone off.'

The landlord came back, this time carrying three plates of steak and kidney pie.

'I've given them some of your specials, John,' he said.

'Yes, yes, alright,' snapped Mr Hall, and again the landlord retreated.

As we ate John Hall produced a large folded plan from his coat pocket and opened it on the table. I could see that it was a map of Mr Perkins's farm and the hill we were working on.

He chose a point on the hill and put his finger on it.

'This is where we stood,' he said. He took out a pencil and wrote WE STOOD on the map. Then he swept his hand across the bottom corner.

'This land here's ours,' he said. 'And it needs a new boundary fence. Perkins says it's our responsibility. The lads did some the other day, but they've gone off now.'

He didn't explain why or where they'd gone. He folded the map and pushed it towards me.

'You'll have to do the rest,' he said.

'Does Mr Perkins know you've approached us?' I asked.

'None of his business,' he replied.

I made one more attempt to hold out. 'Our boss won't like it,' I said.

He raised his voice. 'What's the matter with you? You're getting beer, grubbage and cash in hand. What more could you want?'

A couple of people at the bar were now looking in our direction.

I turned to Tam and Richie. 'Alright?'

They both nodded.

'Alright then,' I said to Mr Hall. He grunted and ordered more drinks. So there I was, committed. Which meant we were going to be at Upper Bowland for even longer. I don't think Tam and Richie had thought about this part of the equation. All they were interested in was the cash Mr Hall was going to pay us. As soon as he'd dropped us off at the caravan they began talking as if we were going to land a windfall. They seemed to forget all the extra work we would have to do. Mr Hall was their benefactor, and after all the beer he'd bought them they would not have a word spoken against him.

'We'll be in trouble if Donald finds out,' I said.

'We won't tell him, will we?' replied Tam.

I supposed not. I had to admit the idea of a bit of extra cash in hand was attractive, and if we got stuck in over the weekend we could easily get the work done by Monday.

Even so, I had the usual trouble dragging them out of bed the following morning. We were supposed to meet Mr Hall's brother David along the road at eight o'clock. We needed to get going before that though because the first thing we had to do was go up onto the hill and get our tools. We got to the roadside meeting place on time, and the brother turned up at ten past eight in a small flatbed lorry loaded with posts and wire. He was like a slightly deflated version of John Hall, only much more cheerful. In fact he seemed to have a constant line of banter.

'Hoo hoo!' he chimed through the cab window as he pulled up. 'Beer and skittles, eh lads? Ha ha!'

Tam and Richie took to him instantly, even though he declined the offer of a fag. Personally I thought he went on a bit too much. He kept making jokes about fencing which involved parrying with an imaginary sword and shouting *en garde* every few minutes. As far as our sort of fencing was concerned, I was unable to picture him swinging a post hammer or digging holes. However, he was a pleasant enough bloke, and obliged us by driving the lorry slowly along the proposed fence line while Tam and Richie threw the posts off the back.

The fence itself looked like a straightforward enough piece of work. After David Hall had gone Tam went marching about chanting 'Easy! Easy!' at the top of his voice. He was right, it was easy. But it was also going to be a boring slog. We were used to building fences over sloping land and difficult terrain. That was our speciality after all. This fence, though, just went on and on along the edge of the Hall Brothers' land. It was all flat. There were also a hell of a lot of posts to put in. Unlike the high-tensile fence we were building on the hill, this was a conventional wire-netting job. The posts had to be two yards apart to support the net, which meant there were four hundred of them! By the middle of the afternoon, knocking in post after post after post, the monotony was getting to us. Tam had taken to counting how many posts were already in, and how many were left to do. This seemed to make matters worse.

'That's one hundred and forty seven,' he would announce, as another post was completed. 'Three more and it's a hundred and fifty.'

And so on. I began to wonder if all this was really worth it. The only advantage I could see was that Tam would be solvent again when Mr Hall paid us on Monday. Which would take the pressure off me to keep providing subs, especially as now Richie was running short too, having himself lent so much to Tam. It suddenly struck me that we were expecting to get paid as soon as we finished the work. What if Mr Hall held out for a while before settling up? We hadn't thought of that. I didn't mention the possibility to Tam and Richie in case it affected their workrate. I didn't want them to lose their momentum so that we ended up with two uncompleted jobs on our hands. My suspicions deepened that evening when David Hall came by with several pounds of sausages for us. I hoped the Hall Brothers were not going to try to fob us off by paying us in kind. Tam and Richie, on the other hand, saw the sausages as a bonus, and when we got back to the caravan they began frying them for our tea. 'Did you have to cook the whole lot?' I said, as Tam attended to a fully laden frying pan. He was stabbing the sausages one by one with a fork.

'Yah,' he said. 'There's plenty more where these came from.'

'You think so?'

'I know so. From now on it's gonna be beer and skittles for us.'

'You mean cakes and ale.'

Tam looked at me. 'I know what I fucking mean.'

It took us a while to recover from all those sausages, and the hard day's work, but we eventually made it to the Queen's

Magnus Mills

Head, where the landlord stood us our first round of drinks and told us to call him Ron. It was as if our dealings with Mr Hall had bestowed on us some sort of special status. During the evening Tam and Richie were invited to make up the pub darts team, despite their having shown no previous interest in the game. I was left out, but I tried not to take this as a personal snub. When Tam rolled up his sleeves to play, I again looked at the words 'I mascot' tattooed on his arm. It came as no surprise that Tam's throwing was fairly accurate, while Richie's shots tended to be consistently wayward. It was a passable evening, but when we got home that night it was obvious that I was now the only one with any money left. And it was Saturday tomorrow.

Geoff Ryman

253

'A triumph of imagination.'   *New Statesman*

A Bakerloo line tube train with no one standing and no empty seats carries 252 passengers. The driver makes 253. They all have their own secret histories, their own thoughts about themselves and their travelling neighbours. And they all have one page, totalling exactly 253 words, devoted to them. Each page a story, each page a novel. There are connections and rejections, chance meetings and frantic avoidance, bitter memories and sweet anticipation.

It's a seven-and-a-half-minute journey between Embankment and the Elephant & Castle. It's the journey of 253 lifetimes . . .

———————

Geoff Ryman is a Canadian writer, author of numerous highly acclaimed works, now living and working in London and Oxfordshire. He works as Head of New Media for the Central Office of Information.

253
Available now from Flamingo
ISBN 0 00 655078 9

THE DRIVER –
MR TAHSIN ÇELIKBILEKLI

Outward appearance
Like Antonio Banderas in *Interview with the Vampire*, down to the long black hair. London Underground uniform, neatly pressed except the jacket which is slung over the back of his chair. Unshaven, baggy-eyed. His Hush Puppy shoes are worn along one edge.

Inside information
A qualified Turkish political scientist living in Britain with a British wife. He walks splay footedly because his feet were beaten while he was in prison. His name means Perfection With Steel Wrists. Turkish surnames are new this century, added under the rule of Ataturk – Father Turk. Such names sound beautiful to them.

What he is doing or thinking
The train pulls out, Tahsin sighs with exhaustion. Last night he argued with his two best friends about Islamic fundamentalism. Tunc teaches at the School of Oriental and African Studies[1] and is from an old Ottoman family. 'There are only a million modern Turks, but we have all the power,' Tunc said, heavy lidded with superiority. Tahsin's other friend Umut is a failed actor, drinking himself to death. 'There would be no more wine,' Umut complained. 'Umut' means Hope. Tahsin lost his temper with both of them.

Tahsin is from Marash, a town famous only for its rubbery ice cream. His mother and father are illiterate and faithful. 'My modern son,' sighs his father on the phone with pride when told Tahsin is writing a book on a computer. After all the other isms, Islam at least feels native.

His jacket is being crushed. Sleepily, Tahsin hangs it on an available peg – the Dead Man's Handle.

Another helpful and informative
253 *footnote*
1 As a service to our international readers, 253 provides these helpful and informative footnotes designed to point out unusual features of history and architecture. Relax! Imagine you are on a whirlwind coach tour of Britain – only without being trapped for two weeks with people you never want to see again.

The School of Oriental and African Studies became part of the University of London in 1916 and is yet to fully become so in spirit. Its original building is a dispiriting brick nonentity lost in the no man's land between Russell Square and Malet Street. A newer extension (1979) looks like the South Bank. A new building was donated by the Sultan of Brunei in the 1990s to the School. It needed it.

Scholars from vastly different disciplines and cultures who live in the suburbs and commute daily discover at SOAS that they have nothing to say to each other. Proof positive that to have geography in common is to have nothing in common.

In fact, SOAS has a lot in common with tourist group bus tours.

Or perhaps a trip on London Underground.

MR ANDRE STANLEY

Outward appearance

Ageing football coach? American letterman's jacket with beige sleeves, black trunk. OSHKOSH INDIANS it announces, NUMBER 22. White Levis jeans, white socks, black shoes, salt and pepper hair, healthy pink complexion. A young person into retro fashion would kill to know where Andre finds his clothes.

Inside information

A minister from an Episcopalian diocese in Wisconsin on a theological fact-finding mission. Andre is particularly bemused by the debate about gay priests. Why the fuss? There are none.

Andre served in Vietnam. He is baffled by all the talk of post-traumatic stress disorder. He piloted helicopters and saw the worst the war had to offer – the blasted bodies of young men – but he has no trouble accounting for the deaths, the destruction. God leaves everyone free, everyone responsible, even Nazis. We are free to wage mistaken wars, mistranslate the Bible, or commit rapes. And we are free to fight back.

Andre wants to write screenplays for Jesus ... and reclaim the media from barnstorming fundamentalists. He is working on a screen treatment now, about helicopter pilots in Vietnam.

What he is doing or thinking

Trying not to breathe. The man next to him stinks beyond belief. It is an inhuman smell, very pungent, like scorched hops. It reminds Andre of his one visit to the Annhauser-Busch brewery in Los Angeles, which was like a sewer. Do all English people smell like this? Don't they ever wash? Maybe they just don't know about dry cleaning.

Then a woman says in exasperated, fruity tones: 'This is unbearable! Can't you use a deodorant?'

Outward appearance

John Carradine? Elongated, raffish, middle-aged man. An ill-fitting black overcoat. Its velvet collar arches up to his hair line. Bone-thin, hairy wrists. Young person's black, thick-soled shoes.

Inside information

Purchaser for Mosstains and closet novelist. Sits alone in his office and continually rewrites *Pastel Images*, a novel based on a love affair he had in 1967.

Kevin would not recognize himself under the lank grey hair. Being a kind of handsome and full of promise was part of his identity for so long that it comes as a shock to realize he is near retirement, without a published novel or even a chain of mistresses. As if his life were not complicated enough, under the black suit, he is wearing women's underwear.

What he is doing or thinking

Kevin wonders with hurt bafflement why his career has stalled. Colleagues avoid him; salesmen cancel appointments. His PA keeps her window wide open. The office is freezing. 'Do you have to keep the window open all the time?' he once asked. Her face was hard, strange. 'We need the air,' she replied. His nick-name around the office is Rotten Fish. All of this is very hurtful. He is a sensitive, creative person.

To his horror the woman sitting next to him erupts, jowls quivering. 'This is unbearable,' she announces. 'Can't you use a deodorant? You smell like a bonfire of old rubber tyres!'

What is she talking about? Kevin can't help sniffing; he smells nothing. Insulted, hypnotized by shock, he stands to get off one stop early at Waterloo.

MS CORRINE TRACY

Outward appearance

Stylish black woman, late twenties. Long one-piece dress in a brown herring-bone pattern, brown overcoat with hood, matching flat-heeled boots. Hair short, combed forward, simple gold earrings. Handbag on floor.

Inside information

Works for Winona Hairdressers just behind the Elephant and Castle. She is now the only hairdresser left in the shop, which is seeing hard times.

What she is doing or thinking

Why does everyone assume a black hairdresser can only do black hair? Corrine has photographs of white ladies in her window as well. She's grateful to her black customers, but there aren't enough of them. She spends the better part of most working days staring into space. She is so bored.

She's taken to designing toys, with some success. Leap Frog was a spring-driven wooden toy that jumped. Her brother managed to sell the patent for that. She has been trying to design Scissors Crab, a plastic crab with goofy eyes on springs and pincers that can cut paper. The problem has been safety.

Corrine muses on other useful things the pincers could do – like knit. Suddenly something moves inside her head. She sees the pincers weaving hair, spinning strands, making braids.

People buy cornrows, they spend hours braiding it, it costs a fortune . . . Corrine covers her mouth. Cornrow Crab, the hair-braider! Inexpensive, do it yourself at home. She reaches into her handbag to pull out her notebook. It isn't there. She pauses, then decides. Sod the job, she's getting back to her design pad. She stands up to get off at Lambeth North instead of the Elephant.

MRS JULIE TILDSLEY

Outward appearance
The last to get on at Embankment, as the doors close. She's youngish, about thirty, but rumpled hair and baggy eyes make her look older and a bit grumpy. She drops down into an empty seat and stares. She wears a shiny white dress.

Inside information
Works for FSD Courier Service near the Elephant. Takes bookings, fills in forms, contacts couriers, gives customers instructions. She lives near Aldgate East – a long way to come, but a job is a job, even one you could do in your sleep.

What she is doing or thinking
Julie actually is asleep. Her morning routine is so established that she dressed herself sleepwalking. She walked on automatic pilot to the tube and changed trains at Embankment without waking up. She is conscious of nothing until Passenger 46 clumps Passenger 47. She thinks: I'm dreaming that I'm sitting on the tube and a man comes in with a bicycle seat and hits a large black man with it. A spooky black lady smiles, nursing something terrible in a parcel. Mick Hucknall seems to be sitting next to the women, singing.

Gradually, Julie realizes it is not a dream. She really is sitting on the tube fingering her white dress. The FSD uniform is a grey skirt.

She's only wearing a slip. Oh my God! she thinks and sits up as the train slows into Waterloo. I'm not dressed, I've got to go home!

All the way to Aldgate East and then walking up Commercial Road, wearing only a slip. But this time she won't be asleep.

MISS FLORENCE CASSELL

Outward appearance

Gamine, Italianate, tiny. Olive skin, curly hair cut short, lots of freckles. Handsome coat with black leather sleeves, and diamond patterns of different coloured leather. Picks disconsolately at its surface.

Inside information

Came to England from Kenya when she was a little girl. From time to time people made comments. Manages an Oddbins; shares a flat with a college friend near Elephant and Castle. Has spent the night with friends after a crisis.

What she is doing or thinking

It started with continual trouble from minicab drivers. They would pull over and ask if she wanted to have some fun. One of them showed up on her doorstep and asked her out. She turned him down and he left with reasonably good grace.

Last night the same driver showed up to take her to friends in Queen's Park. She refused to go with him. 'Look, I'm just here for the fare,' he said, affronted. They ended up driving across London in brooding silence. Parked outside her friends' flat he said, 'There. All safe and sound.' Then he said, 'And listen you half-caste bitch, just 'cause you got some white in you doesn't make you any better than anyone else.'

That's all. It was enough.

She spent the evening in the bathroom looking at her face. She had always seen it in her face, but thought her mother would have told her if were true. Why wouldn't her mother tell her? It doesn't make any difference, it shouldn't make any difference. And yet it does, and yet it always does.

Geoff Ryman

MR ALLAN MARJORAM

Outward appearance

Bearded man in a suit and waterproof bunched around his burgeoning body. Oversize head, spectacles, white hands, scuffed shoes. Hunched over *Time Out*, with two different coloured markers. Holds both tops in his mouth.

Inside information

Works in the Foreign and Commonwealth Office Library on Stamford Street. Lives in Harrow with his parents. He is 32 years old.

What he is doing or thinking

Inspecting the *Time Out* personal ads with methodical diligence. His priorities are written on an envelope held underneath each ad. *Red: Short term, pref exotic. Green: Partner, first time advertiser.*

He circles an ad in red.

Attractive Black Woman, 33, graduate professional mature seeks gallant gentleman 33–45, professional, warm hearted ...

He havers. It would be unfair to pretend he was looking for a permanent relationship with a black woman. Besides, he is one year too young. He puts a question mark.

Green Eyes, Red Hair Lady 30 trendy (ish) creative job WLTM sexy man with GSOH for warm nights in. Photo please.

He promptly circles this in green. It meets all his requirements. He's not sexy, though. On second thought, he changes the colour to red.

Allan wishes someone would tell him what a GSOH was. And why did so many people want someone who speaks Chinese or Arabic?

Woman, 32, part-Jewish, sharp tongued seeks someone understanding . . .

That sounded a bit fierce.

Cute half-Italian lady, 35, seeks affectionate, understanding, trustworthy guy . . .

Green. That's all there are. He ranks the greens in order of preference. The train slows and he takes the pen tops out of his mouth.

The 253
Personal Ads

WHAT YOU *REALLY* NEED OTHER PEOPLE FOR!

Masculine fruit and veg man, 35, GSOH, going to seed, often wears no shirt seeks female customers to be mildly titillated and buy his cucumbers. Full price list available on request.

Swings both ways ... male or female makes no difference to this post office counter worker who seeks lunchtime relief. Low pay means he's all alone on the afternoon shift. Help him cut that queue! A burden shared is a burden shared.

Dry cleaning shop seeks woman, pref Eastern-European speaking, for below minimum wage employment. Must have unrecognized degree from university in collapsed republic and charming, intelligent, hardworking manner.

Man, 39, told good looking, needs someone to tell him he's good looking. That's all.

Professional male, handsome but ditsy 32, seeks adult to return library books, get printer in for repair, pay council tax etc. Most letters with photograph answered unless lost. Must be prepared to answer all other responses to this ad.

Woman, 40, needs people to mother. Preferably lower class and ignored at work. Let me do everything for you. That way we can never be equals. All nationalities welcome.

Middle-aged woman, non-scene, seeks same for visiting Royal Academy Summer Show, exchanging gardening tips etc. Must drink Earl Grey. No phonies.

Married couple mid-30s seek new friends for safe times at pop concerts. Lightning Seeds, Boo Radleys. Full and frank letter stating preferences gets same by return.

Young 50, isolated, needs devoted listeners for monotone political rants: Clinton a commie, Thatcher destroyed country etc. Willing to travel.

LEON DE MARCO

Outward appearance
Skinny young man, Italian pallor, 1960s pointed boots, brown leather jacket on coat-hanger shoulders, pink shirt with black bead patterns embroidered on it. Sits scrunched up against the section divider, legs crossed at ankles, face bitter with fatigue. Suddenly smiles gently at Passenger 121.

Inside information
Leon has been out all night. Lives on an estate on Hercules Road[2] with his mum. She will already have gone to work, leaving an anxious note to ring her.

What he is doing or thinking
Remembering last night. Went with his mates to *Wet*, a new club, and stayed 'til 5.00 A M. *Wet* has a temporary swimming pool set up in it. Everyone strips down to their shorts, the girls take off their tops, it's cool, nobody gets hassled. It's just so much fun to dance until you're sweaty, and then to swim. It was sexy but nobody got groped. Well not badly. They all just talked.

He can't remember what it was about, but it was light and heavy at the same time: stars, the beginning of the universe, how good everybody looked. And don't swallow the water.

Then out, feeling glossy, cool, fresh, round to a caff by the market for coffee and doughnuts. They loved each other, at least when they said goodnight, see ya, with the birds beginning to sing in the trees.

He wishes he could hold it in place, build some kind of monument to it. The train slows at Lambeth North and he moves towards the pigeon. 'Come on, little pigeon, go on home,' he says.

Another helpful and informative
253 *footnote*
2 According to Graham Gibberd's *On Lambeth Marsh*, land bounded by the current Hercules Road, Kennington Road and Cosser Street was leased by Sergeant Major Philip Astley in the 1780s. There he built his own house, Hercules Hall, the Hercules Tavern, and also Hercules Terrace, where William Blake[2a] lived. Until redecoration in 1996/97 the pub was a kind of branch office of the Central Office of Information, serving fine spirits, hot and cold dishes and eczema. The Central Office of Information, on Hercules Road, is decorated with a crude mosaic of the labours of Hercules, doubtless in some ignorance of Astley.

The Sergeant Major was a circus strongman, who performed 'Twelve Trials of Hercules' in his own theatre, Astley's. The amphitheatre was on the site of the current St Thomas' Hospital nurses' home on Westminster Bridge Road. Astley's son took it over, and it remained in operation for many years, part of the Lambeth tradition of cheap theatrical spectacle that continues to this day with shameful excesses such as the Royal National Theatre.

Dickens describes the vulgarity of the crowd and the inferiority of the spectacle at Astley's in *Sketches by Boz*.

Astley's went through a number of name changes, often like the National called 'Royal', and remained open until 1893. It was finally closed, like so many buildings south of the river, for being a disorderly house.

Read the tea leaves, National.

A helpful and informative **253** *footnote* within *a footnote*
2a On 11th January 1995, William Blake came back to Hercules Road.

The train, trailing spirits, pulled him. He arrived staggering forward as if hurled onto the platform of Lambeth North tube station. He swirled, like the leaves the Council no longer sweeps up, that rattle undead on the streets year after year.

Outward appearance
He wears a broad, squashed straw hat and a compress for a toothache. His jacket is long and brown, stained, but he wears a new cravat, snow white. His tan breeches down to the knee have not been changed all winter, and the stockings, his silken best, are splattered with clay and dung two hundred years old.

It is how he was dressed on 11th January 1795.

So who is William Blake?
The year just past, 1794, has been his annus mirabilis. Out of his tiny cottage he has written, illustrated, printed *Songs of Experience*, the *Book of Urizon, Europe: A Prophecy* and the *Book of Los*. He is

exhausted. To clear his head, he went walking down Leake Street, under the tossed trees, past cows fenced in the fields of Kennington Manor. Battered by the wind, he was returning when his body was caught up in a mightier gust of the spirit.

What he is doing or thinking
He comes to a stop, and clutches his toothache and looks around him.

It is another vision. He is prone to them. In this vision, people walk through some dim, chattering tunnel. There are black ropes from the ceiling and a terrible smell he cannot identify. It reminds him of the charred odour of the Albion Mill. Dark, satanic, burned in fear and anger by the people, it stinks on in Lambeth Marsh.

A vision of Albion, then, of the spirit of that scorched mill.

The air is dim and terrible. The people scurry as if pursued. He allows himself to be blown along with them, up the tunnel. He wonders: what sad spirits are these? In what echoing bowels of Urizon are they trapped, shuffling? Their clothes are strange. He cannot quite focus on them, the materials, the colours, the cut are so alien to him. But he has learned that in visions detail is all. As in life, the solid details are emanations of the spirit.

He follows two handsome black wenches. So imposing and so spangled with jewellery are they, that it seems to him they must be princesses from some dream kingdom. One talks animatedly. The other, evidently her superior, looks away. Lord, such savage majesty!

They have blue painted on their eyelids! The inferior woman clutches a bag of miraculous tissue that contains, in its satin translucence, useful household objects which Blake recognizes. They warm his heart in a way he does not understand.

They mount steps, into another ghostly chamber, and line up, faces dead, waiting in acquiescence before polished iron gates. Is there fire beyond them?

They are joined by an elderly woman, gazing at flowers. A man, even older, asks her, 'Can I interest you in a further beverage?' His voice is richly grandiose. It is a tone of voice that Blake heard in his own age. He hates it for its aggrandisement. Yet, for all his vocal majesty, there is something glinting and small about this friendly old man. Blake somehow understands that his sonorousness is a final, sad crumbling of former grandeur.

The woman with the flowers looks up, and smiles. Blake realizes that she and all the women here have painted on another face. Has he stumbled on some kind of theatre? The new arrivals all laugh.

A youth joins them, as callow-faced as a Sicilian. His smooth, unharried features are those of a child. Blake peers at him and sees the child is in fact a man in full maturity, though skinny, unbent, with such a delightful expression. The manchild smiles slightly, his face illumined from within by love. Blake wonders if this beauty is to be his angel guide.

Then Blake sees the shoes. The angel manchild is wearing what look like pillows, blue and white. His

Geoff Ryman

trousers are heavy and spongy, without warp and weft. They hang like a single mossy deposit rather than cloth. No one ever wore such clothes in Heaven or in Lambeth. Blake begins to appreciate the scale of what has befallen him.

The doors rumble open, as heavily as gates of hell. There is nothing to do but stumble forward.

In clouds of perfume. These people smell variously of mint, sandalwood, almonds, as if the breath of Araby had wafted into this strange carriage with them. They press together in the tiny chamber, the doors close, they are all trapped without a single eye for the wind. But there is no odour of human closeness. The clothes are as spotless as the faces are burnished. The old man bearing whisky laughs with all his teeth intact, as pearly as a young maiden's. A China woman, as if all humankind had called a Parliament underground, is dressed just like Blake's angel, though she is old and female.

The room moves, everything shivering slightly. It is borne upwards, clanking. They are indeed underground, Blake is now sure. There are signs on the walls. They look, at first, like Blake's own poems, portrait-shaped rectangles of melded images and fiery words.

The all-singing musicAL
    JOLSON

WINTER BREAKAWAYS

The room slumps slightly as if tired. The people shuffle in place, the doors rumble open. To Blake's great relief, there is daylight flooding the tiled chambers beyond. Blake follows his angel who strides so confidently forward.

Straight ahead there is an arch and a blaze of light on grey. In that winter light, suddenly hurtling past are armouries of metal. They hiss, roar past the opening, in heraldic reds, blues, greens. The armouries are as polished as the people as if the devil had been freshly minting folk as well as coins.

In front of him clattering devices applaud, lights flash, barring his way. *Please seek assistance*

Words of fire? Blake looks around him.

The people disperse, quickly, purposively. They ignore him. Where is his angel guide?

Damn ye, thinks Blake and leaps the barriers. He strides on, following the boy, out through the arch, across paving, onto a polished slate surface.

Into a place of permanent winter. Everything grey, everything paved, under stone, as if the people were swept up at night. There is a harsh cleanliness in the air. All the perfumes of Araby cannot make it wholesome. There are no fresh scents of river, lime trees, manure, straw, or laundry airing on the marsh. Instead there is a stench, like tar or oil lamps.

Underfoot symbols zig-zag across the slate. Are they hieroglyphs? Blake stands transfixed in the middle of the road.

Lined up, the armouries have been waiting, rumbling. Suddenly, they all leap forward, heads down, charging towards him. Blake stands dazed, raising his cane against them. All the armouries bellow and beep.

He feels himself grabbed. His angel manchild has him by the sleeve and hauls him up, onto some kind of island of safety amid the slate.

The angel manchild says: 'You all right, mate?' *Please seek assistance* the fire had said.

Blake feels himself to be slack, bewildered, peering at the boy. What hundreds of years could go into the making of that voice? It is a London voice, it is the sound of the mudlark children in the clay flats herding their goats, selling their dung. And yet. This voice is also urbane, polished, fed to bursting as any aristocrat's.

The boy glances at the cane. 'You need a hand across the road?'

'Aye, indeed, or I fear I shall be squashed flatter than a flea between my mistress's thumb and fingernail.'

The boy blinks at him, then chuckles. 'I guess so.'

'Where be we, boy, what place is this?'

'Well, that there's Hercules Road.'

'Herc . . .' and Blake falls silent.

The human mind is not built for logic, one thing at a time in orderly progression. It is built to swallow things whole and leap to conclusions. Blake sees the Hercules Tavern. Amid the roaring traffic he looks down a street whose slight curve is familiar and sees the names of inns: Red Lion, Crown and Cushion. Where he used to drink.

Without logic, full of dread, Blake asks, 'What year is this?'

The boy tells him.

On Hercules Terrace, William Blake lived in a cottage with his wife Catherine, and he gave the place and the spirit of it a name. 'Beulah . . .'

says the old man. 'I . . . I lived here once.'

'Was B . . . Beulah the name of the estate?' the young man asks him.

'Yes,' replies Blake. Here, he and Catherine would read poetry naked but for their hats, and answer the door in that pure condition. 'It was an age ago.'

Leon de Marco stares at the old man and at his dress, and he too is moving faster than logic. 'Are you a poet or something?'

'Or something.' Blake finds the idea both apt and amusing. 'Indeed.'

Leon takes hold of William Blake's arm. 'We used to have a poet live here. A famous poet. They put up a plaque.'

'Did they? Well it saved paying him while he was alive.' As if there had been some kind of signal, all the armouries have stalled, and the boy insists that they cross the road now, by pulling Blake's sleeve.

The Hercules Tavern is now all blue, and square. When did all the world stop building sloping roofs? Along Hercules Road, small trees sigh in the wind. 'Are those cherry trees?' Blake asks.

'Yeah.'

'The authorities plant cherry trees, for everyone?'

'I guess so.'

'The petals fall in spring?'

Leon smiles. 'Yeah,' he chuckles. He's always liked that, ever since he was a kid.

'Mark them well, boy, for that is how we all fall, in beautiful lost clouds, thousands of us as if in an upward fall of snow.'

And Blake remembers the creak of

Geoff Ryman

the windmill as it turned beside the brewery. He remembers the clay flats being mined, the diggers shovelling up clay into the oxcarts, the beasts relishing the mud. Across the pistachio river, up the opposite banks of shale, were the long wooden warehouses in front of the modest Parliament chambers. The market for stone and timber. The sounds of saws and the smells of wood and stone dust reached them even across the river. The long barges rested as if asleep, all in front of the Archbishop's great house.

'Are the mills gone? And the factories?'

'Oh,' said the boy. 'No factories any more. All gone.'

'All gone?' says Blake, overjoyed. 'All gone!' He feels his horsey, ruined teeth are betrayed by his grin. 'Was there dancing?'

Leon smiles at him. 'There's always dancing in London, mate.'

Blake can see him clearly now. Blake remembers the Artichoke Inn, on the muddy lane through Lambeth Marsh, and the village maids and the lusty lads outside it, dancing in a ring. This is not an angel, but a lusty Lambeth lad with spots on his chin.

He sees a woman, in middle age with brazen many-coloured hair, wearing what looks like a new bottle-green coat. Her hard glossy shoes have tiny spikes that make her trip slightly as she battles against the lowland wind. She walks like a lady of promise and stature, alone and undefended on the street. He looks at the jumble of buildings, some shiny like wrapped presents, others like wedding cakes, still others like lavatories with tiles. A mighty age, and a confused and fearful one. What achievements had been squandered here?

'Not quite Jerusalem,' says Blake.

He turns and sees the poet's plaque, on a brick wall that is not altogether out of place amid the Georgian houses. *William Blake Poet and Painter lived here . . .*

Beulah. It is remembered. But why?

There is a gust of wind, smelling of river water, mud, hops, sweat, wool and baked bread. Suddenly Leon de Marco is standing alone in Hercules. In the middle of January, clouds of cherry blossom fall billowing upwards from the single line of trees.

Michael Marshall Smith

One of Us

'First class . . . weird, wonderful, gripping. Raymond Chandler
meets Terry Pratchett and they get along fine.' *Daily Express*

Hap Thompson — ex-barman, ex-hood and ex-husband — has fallen
on his feet at last. He's finally found something he can do better than
anyone else. And it's legal. Almost.

Hap's a REMtemp, working the night hours caretaking people's
dreams and memories. One night he takes on a bigger memory than
usual and the client disappears. As Hap pursues her, he comes to
realize that something terrible lies at the end of the memory, something
which threatens to rewrite not just his life, but the whole of history . . .

Michael Marshall Smith's debut novel was the groundbreaking *Only
Forward*. His second novel, *Spares*, is in development with Stephen
Spielberg's production company Dreamworks SKG and Warner
Brothers have bought the film rights for *One of Us* amid intense
competition. His novels are bestsellers in translation around the world.
Michael lives in North London, where he is currently working on
his fourth novel, a collection of short stories, and a number of film
projects while providing a warm place for his cats to sleep.

One of Us
Available now from HarperCollins
ISBN 0 00 649997 X

I GOT INTO it the same way as most people, I guess. By accident.

It was a year and a half ago. I was staying the night in Jacksonville, mainly because I didn't have anyplace else to be. At the time it seemed like whenever I couldn't find a road to take me anywhere new, I wound up back in that city, like a yo-yo bouncing back to the hand that threw it away in the first place. I was planning on getting out of Florida the next day, and after my ride set me down I headed for the blocks round the bus station, where everything costs less. Last time I'd worked had been two weeks ago, at a bar down near Cresota Beach, where I grew up. They didn't like the way I talked to the customers. I didn't care for their attitude towards pay and working conditions. It had been a brief relationship.

I walked the streets until I found a place going by the inspiring and lyrical name of 'Pete's Rooms'. The guy behind the desk was wearing one of the worst shirts I've ever seen, like a painting of a road accident done by someone who had no talent but an awful lot of paint to use up. I didn't ask him if he was Pete, but it seemed a fair assumption. He looked like a Pete. The rate was fifteen dollars a night, Net access in every room. Very reasonable – yet the shirt, unappealing though it was, looked like it had been made on purpose. Maybe I should have thought about that, but it was late and I couldn't be bothered.

My room was on the fourth floor and small, and the air

smelled like it had been there since before I was born. I pulled something to drink from my bag, and dragged the room's one tatty chair over to the window. Outside was a fire escape the rats were probably afraid of using, and below that just yellow lights and noise.

I leaned out into humid night and watched people walking up and down the street. You see them in every big city, mangy dogs sniffing for a trail their instincts tell them must start around here someplace. Some people believe in God, or UFOs: others that just round a corner will be the first step on a road towards money, or drugs, or whatever Holy Grail they're programmed for. I wished them well, but not with much hope or enthusiasm. I'd tried most types of MAKE $$$ FAST!!! schemes by then, and they had got me precisely nowhere. Roads that begin just around corners have a tendency to lead you right back to where you started.

Though I grew up in Florida, I'd spent most of the previous decade on the West Coast, and I missed it. For the time being I couldn't go back, which left me with nowhere in particular to be. It felt like everything had ground to a halt, as if it would take something pretty major to get my life started up again. Reincarnation, maybe. It had felt that way before, but not quite so bleakly. It was the kind of situation that could get you down.

So I lay on the bed and went to sleep.

I woke up early the next morning, feeling strange. Spacey. Hollow-stomached, and as if someone had put little scratchy balls of crumpled paper inside my eyes. My watch said it was seven o'clock, which didn't make sense. The only time I see seven a.m. is when I've been awake straight through.

Then I realized an alarm was going off, and saw that the console in the bedside table was flashing. 'Message' it said. I screwed my eyes up tight and looked at it again. It still said I had a message. I hit the receive button. The screen went blank for a moment, and then fed up some text.

'You could have earned $367.77 last night,' it read. 'To learn more, come by 135 Highwater today. Quote reference pr/43.'

Then it spat out a map. I picked it up; squinted at it.

$367.77 is a lot of nights' bar tending.

I changed my shirt and left the hotel.

By the time I reached Highwater I was already losing interest. My head felt fuzzy and dry, as if I'd spent all night doing math in my sleep. A big part of me just wanted to score breakfast somewhere and go sit on a bus, watch the sun haze on window panels until I was somewhere else.

But I didn't. I have a kind of shambling momentum, once I'm started. I followed the streets on the map, surprised to find myself getting closer to the business district. The kind of people who spam consoles in cheap hotels generally work out of virtual offices, but Highwater was a wide road with a lot of grown-up buildings on either side. 135 itself was a mountain of black plate glass, with a revolving door at the bottom. Unlike many of the other buildings I'd passed, it didn't have exterior videowalls extolling with tiresome thoroughness the virtues and success of the people who toiled within. It just sat there, not giving anything away. I went in, as much as anything just to find some shade.

The lobby was similarly uncommunicative, and likewise decked out all in black. I walked across the marble floor to a desk at the far end, my heels tapping in the cool silence. A woman sat there in a pool of yellow light, looking at me with a raised eyebrow.

'Can I help you?' she asked, her tone making it clear she thought it was unlikely.

'I was told to come here and quote a reference.'

I speak better than I look. Her face didn't light up or anything, but she tapped a button on her keyboard and turned her eyes to the screen. 'And that is?'

I told her, and she scrolled down through some list for a while. 'Okay,' she said. 'Here's how it is. Two options. The first is I give you $171.39, and you go away with no further obligation. The second is that you take the elevator on the right and go up to the 34th floor, where Mr Stratten will meet with you presently.'

'And you arrive at $171.39 how, exactly?'

'Your potential earnings less a twenty-five-dollar handling fee, divided by two and rounded up to the nearest cent.'

'How come I only get half the money?'

'Because you're not on contract. You go up and meet Mr Stratten, maybe that will change.'

'And in that case I get the full $367?'

She winked. 'You're kind of bright, aren't you?'

The elevator was very pleasant. Tinted mirrors, low lights; quiet, leisurely. It spoke of money, and lots of it. Not much happened during the journey.

When the doors opened I found myself faced with a corridor. A large chrome sign on the wall said 'REM temps', in a suitably soul-destroying typeface. Underneath it said, 'Sleep Tight. Sleep *Right*.' I walked the way the sign pointed and ended up at another reception desk. The girl had a badge which said she was Sabrina, and her hair was done up in a weirdly complex manner, doubtless the result of several hours of some asswipe stylist's attention.

I'd thought the girl downstairs was a top-flight patronizer, but compared to Sabrina she was servility itself. Sabrina's manner suggested I was some kind of lower-echelon vermin: lower than a rat, for sure, maybe on a par with a particularly ill-favoured vole, and after thirty seconds with her I felt the bacteria in my stomach start to join in sneering at me. She told me to take a seat, but I didn't. Partly to annoy her, but mainly because I

Michael Marshall Smith

hate sitting in receptions. I read somewhere it puts you in a subordinate position right off the bat. I'm great at the pre-hiring tactics – it's just a shame it goes to pieces afterwards.

'Mr Thompson, good morning. I'm Stratten.'

I turned to see a man standing behind me, hand held out. He had a strong face, black hair starting to silver on the temples. Like any other tall middle-aged guy in a sober suit, but more polished: as if he was a release-standard human instead of the beta versions you normally see wandering around. His hand was firm and dry, as was his smile.

I was shown into a small room off the main corridor. Stratten sat behind a desk, and I lounged back in the other available chair.

'So what's the deal?' I asked, trying to sound relaxed. There was something about the guy opposite which put me on edge. I couldn't place his accent. East Coast somewhere, probably, but flattened, made deliberately average – like an actor covering his past.

He leaned forward and turned the console on the desk to face me. 'See if there's anything you recognize,' he said, and pressed a switch. The console chittered and whirred for a moment, and flashed up 'PR/43 @ 18/5/2016'.

The screen bled to black, and then faded up again to show a corridor. The camera – if that's what it was – walked forward along it a little way. Drab green walls trailed off into the distance. On the left-hand side was another corridor. The camera turned – and showed that it was exactly the same. Going a little quicker now, it tramped that way for a while, before making another turn into yet another identical corridor. There didn't seem to be any shortage of corridors, or of new turnings to make. Occasional chips in the paint relieved the monotonous olive of the walls, but other than that it just went on and on and on.

I looked up after five minutes to see Stratten watching me. I shook my head. Stratten made a note on a piece of paper, and then typed something rapidly on the console's keyboard. 'Not very distinctive,' he said. 'I don't think the donor's very imaginative. And you lose a great deal, just getting the visual. Try this.'

The picture on the screen changed, and showed a pair of hands holding a piece of water. I know 'piece of water' doesn't make much sense, but that's what it looked like. The hands were nervously fondling the liquid, and a quiet male voice was relayed from the console's speaker.

'Oh, I don't know,' it said, doubtfully. 'About five? Six and a half, maybe?'

The hands put the water down on a shelf, and picked up another bit. This water was a little smaller. The voice paused for a moment, then spoke more confidently. 'Definitely a two. Two and a third at most.'

The hands placed this second piece down on top of the first. The two bits of water didn't meld, but remained distinct. One hand moved out of sight and there was a different sound then, a soft metallic scraping. That's when I got my first twitch.

Stratten noticed. 'Getting warmer?'

'Maybe,' I said, leaning to get a closer look at the console. The point of view had swivelled slightly, to show a battered filing cabinet. One of the drawers was open, and the hands were carefully picking up pieces of water – which I now saw were arrayed all around, in piles of differing sizes – and putting them one by one into different drop files. Every now and then the voice would swear to itself, take out one of the pieces of water and return it to a pile – not necessarily the one it had originally come from. The hands started moving more and more quickly, putting water in, taking water out, and all the time there was this low background noise of the voice reciting different numbers.

I stared at the screen, losing awareness of the office around me and becoming absorbed. I forgot that Stratten was even there, and it was largely to myself that I eventually spoke.

'Each of the pieces of water has a different value, not based on size. Somewhere between one and twenty-seven. Each drawer in the filing cabinet has to be filled with the same value of water, but no-one told him how to figure out how much each piece is worth.'

The screen went blank, and I turned my head to see Stratten smiling at me. 'You remember,' he said.

'That was the dream I had just before I woke up. What the fuck's going on?'

'We took a liberty last night,' he said. 'The proprietor of the hotel you stayed in has an arrangement with us. We subsidize the cost of his rooms, and provide the consoles.'

'Why?' I reached unthinkingly into my pocket and pulled out a cigarette. Instead of shouting at me or pulling a gun, Stratten simply opened a drawer and gave me an ashtray.

'We're always looking for new people, people who need money and aren't too fussy about how they get it. This is the best way we've found of locating them.'

'Great, so you found me. And so?'

'I want to offer you a job as a REMtemp.'

'You're going to have to unpack that for me.'

He did. At some length. This is the gist:

A few years previously someone had found a way of taking dreams out of people's heads in real time. A device placed near the head of a sufficiently well-off client could keep an eye out for electromagnetic fields of particular types, and divert the mental states of which they were a function out of the dreamer's unconscious mind and into an erasing device. The government wasn't keen on the idea, but the inventors had hired an attorney trained in Quantum Law, and no-one was really sure what the legal position was any more. 'It depends' was as near as they could get. In the meantime a covert industry was born.

The obvious trade was in nightmares, but they don't happen

very often, and clients balked at buying systems which they only needed every couple of months. They'd only pay on a dream-by-dream basis, and the people who'd developed the technology wanted more return on their investment. Also, nightmares aren't usually so bad, and if they are, they're generally giving you information you could do with knowing. If you're scared crapless about something, there's often a good reason for it.

So gradually the market shifted to anxiety dreams instead. Kind of like nightmares, but not usually as frightening, these are the dreams you get when you're stressed, or tired, or fretting about something. Often they consist of minute and complex tasks which the dreamer has to endlessly go through, not really understanding what they're doing and constantly having to restart. Then just when you're starting to get a grip on what's going on, you slide into something else, and the whole cycle starts again. They usually commence just after you've gone to sleep — in which case they'll screw up your whole night — or in the couple of hours before waking. Either way you wake up feeling tired and worn out, in no state to start a working day when it feels like you've already just been through one.

Anxiety dreams are much more frequent than nightmares, and tend to affect precisely the kind of middle and high management executives who were the primary market for dream disposal. The guys who owned the technology changed their pitch, rewrote the copy in their brochures, and started making some serious money.

But there was a problem.

It turned out that you couldn't just erase dreams. That wasn't the way it worked. Over the course of eighteen months the company started getting more and more complaints, and in the end they worked out what was going on.

When you erase a dream, all you destroy is the imagery, the visuals which would have played over the dreamer's inner eye.

The substance of the dream, an intangible quality which seemed impossible to isolate, remains. The more dreams a client has removed, the more this substance is left behind: invisible, indestructible, but carrying some kind of weight. It hangs around in the room the dream has been erased in, and after thirty or so erasures it gets to the point where the room becomes uninhabitable. It's like walking into a thunderstorm of competing subconscious impulses – absolutely silent but impossible to bear. After a few weeks, the dreams seem to coalesce still further, making the air so thick that it becomes impossible to even enter the room at all.

Unfortunately, the kind of client who could afford dream disposal was exactly the type who was turned on by litigation. After the company had swallowed a few huge out-of-court settlements on bedrooms which were now impassable, they turned their minds to finding a way out of the problem. They tried diverting the dreams into storage data banks, instead of just erasing them. This didn't work either. Some of the dream still seeped out of the hard disks, regardless of how air-tight the casing.

Then finally it clicked. The dreams weren't being used up. Maybe if they were . . .

They gave it a try. A client's transmitting machine was connected to a receiver placed near the bed of a volunteer, and two anxiety dreams were successfully diverted from the mind of one to the other. The client woke up nicely rested and full of vim, ready for another hard day in the money mines. The volunteer had a shitty night of dull dreams he couldn't quite remember, but was paid for his troubles.

No residue was left in the room. The dream was gone. The cash started flowing again.

'And that's what you did to me last night?' I asked, a little pissed at having my mind invaded.

Stratten held up his hands placatingly. 'Trust me, you'll be glad we did. People have varying ability to use up other people's dreams. Most can handle two a night without much difficulty, three at the most. They get up feeling ragged, and drag themselves through the day. Usually they only work every other night – but they still make eight, nine hundred dollars a week. You're different.'

'How's that?' I knew this was most likely a stroke, but didn't care. They didn't come along that often.

'You took four dreams last night without breaking sweat. The two you've just seen, and another two – one of which was so boring I can't bear to even watch just the visuals. You could probably have taken a couple more. You could make a lot of money.'

'How much is a lot?'

'We pay according to dream duration, with additional payments if they're especially complex or tedious. Last night you erased over three hundred dollars' worth – and that doesn't factor in a bonus for the dullest one. Depending how often you worked, you could be earning between two and three thousand dollars. A week.' He closed the pitch. 'And we pay cash. Dream disposal is still in an unstable state with regard to legality, and we find it more convenient to obfuscate the nature of our business to some of the authorities.'

He smiled. I smiled back.

Three thousand dollars is an *awful* lot of bar tending.

It wasn't a difficult decision.

I signed a non-disclosure contract. I was leased a receiver, and had it explained to me. Basically I could go anywhere in the continental United States, as long as I kept the machine within six feet of my head while I was asleep. I didn't have to go to bed at any particular time, because the dreams booked to me were just spooled into memory. As soon as the device sensed I was in REM sleep it fed the backlog into my head. When I got up in the morning my nightwork would be there on the screen like a list of email messages: how long the dreams had been, when they started and finished, and whether they qualified for bonus payment or were just hack work.

And at the bottom of the list, the good news. A figure in dollars. I found I could take six or seven dreams a night without too much difficulty. Some days I'd be groggy and find it difficult to concentrate on anything more complex than smoking, but when that happened I'd just take the following night off.

After six months I was recalled to REMtemps' offices and asked if I'd like to volunteer for a higher proportion of bonus dreams. I said 'Hell, yes', and my earnings took another jump upwards. I met a hacker called Quat in the Net, and hired him to write me a daemon which would circulate my earnings around a variety of virtual accounts: every now and then the IRS or some other ratfink would close in on one of them, but when that happened I'd just swallow the loss and keep the rest of it on the move. I also paid him a lot of money to erase a particular incident from the LAPD's crimebank, which meant I could go back to California.

It was a good life. I travelled from place to place, this time as a person with money instead of someone looking for a score. After a while it came to seem natural to wear better clothes, to head for the upscale hotels. I got used to the other things that money gets you, like a modicum of respect, and bed companions who don't issue you with an invoice in the morning. I kept in touch with the few people I cared about through the phone, the Net and occasional flying visits. I dropped in on Deck in LA a couple times, and the city began to lose its darkness for me. I began to think of moving back there, of letting it be my place once again.

There were occasional downsides. Boredom. The exhaustion

which came after a night full of bonuses, and the emotional flatness from being forever on the move and never having a relationship which lasted longer than a few days. There were periods when I'd go a little weird, and I came to realize that was because I'd spent so many nights having other people's dreams that I hadn't had time for any of my own. When that happened I'd clock off, let my mind catch up and do the subconscious boogie. After a few days I'd be fine again.

I'd found some action which was safe, which I was good at, and which paid big-time money.

That should have been enough.

Michael Marshall Smith

Richard Rayner

Murder Book

'This is a masterpiece . . . Unputdownable.' *Sunday Express*

Murder Book is a brooding, violent and sexy thriller set in Los Angeles, where an apparently routine murder investigation takes on a darker hue when it is discovered the victim was mother to LA's biggest crack dealer and idol of the ghetto. As the *Los Angeles Times* says: '*Murder Book* is neo-neo-noir, a mannerist thriller that shakes free of the period-piece mode of both Ellroy and Walter Moseley. Rayner's book has a '90s kind of bleakness and the multiracial cast of characters adds a welcome contemporary feeling.'

———————

Richard Rayner was born in Yorkshire, and educated in North Wales and at Cambridge. He is the author of *Los Angeles Without a Map*, soon to be a cult film featuring Johnny Depp, and writes for *Granta*, the *New York Times* and *Harper's Bazaar*. He lives in Los Angeles.

Murder Book
Available now from Flamingo
ISBN 0 00 651140 6

MY NAME IS Billy McGrath. I'm forty years old, a little under six feet, and find myself in my office late on this sulphurous Los Angeles night, talking to a tape recorder out of both sides of my mouth. I'm half American, half English – offspring of two nations, two languages, and two different ways of seeing the world. I was conceived in Arizona, born on the sixth floor of Santa Monica Hospital, but made my first confession in England, where I learned to shoot among drystone walls old as Julius Caesar and studied philosophy three years at the university of a northern town dominated by a soot-blackened cathedral on a hill, mediaeval reminder of man's lofty aspiration and worldly impermanence.

It was a scholarship that brought me back to America, to study postgrad at UCLA, though the PhD was already out of the picture by the time I met my wife, from whom I'm now divorced, at Marty McFly's sports bar off Interstate 5 in Burbank with a Jack Daniel's in my hand only three days before she saved my life. We have a kid, a girl, Lucy, and we used to live together in a two-storey house that was painted muddy brown on one of those walk streets in Venice where you can't park a car. After I moved out, my wife had the house remodelled and it's now a pretty blue. I'm a cop, though it's a while since I had anything to do with law and order.

Hanging from the ceiling in my office is a redwood sign that says homicide and has on it a little picture of a smoking gun, a 9 mm, lest I forget. Spinning in my chair, I see the locked filing cabinets that surround my desk on three sides. These cabinets, very different from the wrecked metal models elsewhere in the building, are custom made from pine by a carpenter in Mar Vista, a guy who also makes coffins, as it happens, and, perceiving an appropriate symmetry, offers the Department a rate.

The cabinets gleam and shine; there are eight of them, each six feet high by three feet wide, each containing seven shelves, and each shelf in turn supporting thirty two-inch blue plastic binders, the murder books, the records of every homicide investigation in the precinct. Some have a red dot on the spine – unsolved, still in progress. Those with the yellow dots we've closed: arrived at perpetrator and motive, teased out the causes of obvious or sometimes seemingly random events, brought order if not meaning to bloody chaos. Seven of the cabinets are completely filled. Only the one immediately at my back has any space left in it at all – two empty shelves. At my feet there's an open box containing a stack of handsome new binders, ready to go, but it's behind me that I reach, for one book in particular.

Before opening it, I want to mention that my very first homicide wasn't here, in Venice, but down in South LA, Sixty-fifth and Vernon, a nice-looking wood frame house next to a host of similars, and every one of them had bars on every window. Two victims. First was a black guy, the back of his head taken away by a cross-nosed bullet. Second was his white girlfriend; she'd been shot in the face, and both her arms had been hacked off. The shovel that was used for the job was on the floor amidst a butcher's mess of blood and bone. One skinny white arm lay next to it, and we never did find the other or figure out that particular detail, though the really bad thing was the little girl, a child of mixed blood, two years old and fine, at least not physically hurt. She'd been strapped in her highchair with her mouth taped shut so she couldn't scream while she saw the death of her mother and father.

I was just a rookie, a raw recruit, a *boot*, a uniform at the door trying not to get his feet in the mess, but when I went home that night the soles of my boots were clogged with blood and a dried greyish matter I realized must be brain. I sat at the kitchen table to clean them off and asked myself how such things could happen. I wondered at what point an act became evil. How bad and premeditated did it have to be? I swore that I'd keep in contact with that little girl every six months or so to make sure that she was OK. I made good on the promise until she was a six-year-old with pigtails who still refused to talk, but then for no good reason I can remember I missed an appointment, then another and another, until at last I felt embarrassed to go back.

I don't want to make too much of this, though I think the story, along with my lack of the proper equipment of roots, my missing of that cathedral on a hill, does have a bearing on all that happened. I grew too used to seeing evil done. You begin by trying to make a difference and end by doing it yourself, though even that sounds like casting around. At forty I had twenty years' English and twenty American, which might be to say that I had nothing.

I couldn't say how big that crowd was on Santa Clara Avenue, there was so much rain and so many glistening umbrellas, and people kept jumping, moving, and shuffling in the storm, but I did see that most of the faces were the same, with identical expressions of eager, drenched excitement, all keen to see the show. I saw a black street kid with his head shaved, maybe ten years old, gangstered down in a dripping white T-shirt and baggy, sodden jeans with the crotch almost at his ankles.

'Hey, kid. What's your name?'

'Nelson.' Grinning, he turned to show his buddies that he

wasn't afraid. Rain flicked from his eyebrows and caught me under the chin.

'What's happenin', Nelson? Tell me what's up, man.'

'Some lady got killed.'

'Just one?' I grinned back at him, but Nelson wasn't sure whether I was joking or not. Before he could decide and start acting tough, I'd moved on and was making myself imagine that there was no crowd, that there were none of those thirty or more uniformed guys, milling and looking busy, that I was on my own, trying to figure this out. I tried to sweep away all the clutter and noise, to put my mind in a silent place, as if I were about to step into the woods after dark, and every little thing from now on – each falling leaf or twig that snapped – would have to be recorded and remembered if ever I were to find my way out again.

The house was better than I'd expect in the Oakwood neighbourhood of Venice, with a pair of plump white sofas, a new and expensive carpet, and pale, freshly painted walls. Up above the fireplace was a Jesus in an ebony frame, and beneath it, to the left, on a round glass coffee table, seven or eight family portraits. There was an expensive stereo and five VCRs all hooked up together for copies, and there were lots of CDs, hundreds, maybe even a couple of thousand. Someone in the house was crazy for music. There was a powerful smell that didn't fit – strawberries.

In the kitchen I saw a black woman lying face up, with her head pointing south. She was about fifty and dressed in white – white jogging suit, white socks, expensive white sneakers. Her ankles were tied with white nylon cord, and from the way she was lying bumped up around the waist, I guessed her hands were tied behind her back as well. There were spots above the right trouser knee of the jogging suit, blood specks, like tadpoles with the tails pointing up.

The suit had been yanked open, ripped, and there were burns

on her neck and chest. I counted seven, almost like brands on an animal, still bloody and sore, each the size of a red-hot dime. Could be they'd been made with the angry end of a cigar or cigarette. She'd been shot in the left eye, and blood had dribbled from the nostrils. Her open right eye gazed at the ceiling. The other, the wrecked one, was a mess of red and black, turned inside out like a crushed snail. A thick grey ooze of brain escaped at the corner.

The back door was locked and bolted. On the counter next to the water cooler was a clean spoon and a plastic honey bear lying flat on its belly; two or three drops had leaked out, and the ants, fled inside from the rain, were starting to gather.

The doors to the cupboard under the sink were open. A folded report card sat like a little white tent over the shell casing where it had fallen, beneath the U-bend. Sitting in the sink itself was a black garbage bag, also folded, as if it had come right out of a box. This was odd, since there was a full roll of them up on a spinner by the back door.

I put that little detail away.

Sitting next to, and almost concealed by, the garbage bag, were the strawberries, two untouched trays and a third with just a couple taken. I turned to a uniform standing at the door who told me the victim's name.

Mae Richards.

Maybe some basehead had broken in and got carried away – unlikely, since there was no sign of forced entry or struggle.

Maybe she'd been surprised by a knock at the door, and had opened to invite in some random scumbag posing as a salesman or the guy from the gas company. It happens.

Maybe this was done by someone she knew, to whom she owed a debt or with whom she'd been in love. Very possible. In my work, motives tend to be simple and strong: anger, fear, or love turned sour; and money, of course, always money.

Some cases are dramatic from the start and muscle right into the TV news. Others, the sleepy ones, seemingly more commonplace, merit only a few lines in the local rag, but each, on closer examination, is a story, a melodrama within a mystery. People understand this; hence the fascination, mingled with the fear that they themselves could be killed, and the giddy, almost reassuring, suspicion that they too are capable of murder. Hey, I'll blow your head off, mother*fucker*: these days the almost instinctive response to affront or rage or boredom, an answer like installing cable, but with more lasting if unanticipated personal consequences, and not only for the murderee.

From the distance came a church bell's weary clang. This didn't seem such a special one. I was trying to figure out why there was such a crowd outside when Cataresco and Diamond came in, the duty detectives, Cataresco first, ducking beneath the yellow tape, and then Diamond, who lifted it so he could walk straight under. Cataresco unzipped her leather jacket and met me with a smile. Blond, slender, with a talk-show host's nimble alertness, she had a gift for getting into the minds of suspects. Diamond was squat and square-shouldered, powerful looking, a spiritual Dillinger who exuded boredom like the smell of dry-cleaning fluid. He wore a striped tie and a stiff sports jacket that hung slackly from his shoulders, as if suspended from an iron bar lashed across his upper back, and he thrust a hard paunch in front of him like swag. 'Hey hey hey,' he said, popping a cigarette in his mouth without bothering to light it. 'And to think last night I was almost like a human being. There I was, at home, Johnnie Walker in hand, Pavarotti on the CD. Of course this was while I was with your wife,' he said. 'Must be a surprise to you that she's an opera fan, huh?'

Cataresco rolled her eyes. One of the homicide section's more tedious routines was the pretence that we spent the weekends trying to score with each other's wives, a gag that had no real sting anymore, unless made by Cataresco.

'Knew she liked the opera,' I said. 'Didn't know she was so fond of you.'

At forty-five, Diamond had more years on the job than I did, though I was the one who made head of the section, six weeks previously. The money in our line of work wasn't great; thus our struggles for power and status were intense, though everyone pretended otherwise, with the willed, taut nonchalance cops bring even to the world's most obvious wrongs.

Sniffing, Diamond took the cigarette from his mouth and slid it back with its comrades. 'Yeah, well, anyways,' he said, hitching up his pants to reveal a holstered Marine Corps Colt, a cannon. 'That was yesterday I was with your wife.'

Twin gouts of blood had hardened to a moustache beneath Mae Richards's nostrils. Her sneakered right foot turned in at an angle, as if the bone had snapped. Ants were on the march now up her neck and cheek. Soon they'd gather around the blood and meat of her eye and march back again, bearing their treasure. In my experience dead people never look like they're sleeping. They look like they've been shocked out of their lives, and dropped, dumped bones suddenly no more connected than a bag of parts.

Drew Diamond went on. 'And today here I am, back hanging with the brothers in Oakwood. You missed the party.'

'A gangster shows up, tries to break through the line,' said Cataresco.

'Not just any gangster,' said Diamond.

'Ricky Lee Richards,' said Cataresco.

Diamond did the thing with his pants again, pleased by the effect of the name.

'*That* Ricky Lee Richards?' I asked.

'The very same.'

'The Prince of Darkness?'

'The gangbanging piece of scum.'

Ricky Lee Richards was street-famous, already almost a

legend. He'd entered the drug trade with only $200, supplying rock houses across Los Angeles, before in time becoming a chief cocaine wholesaler, the funnel through which the drug arrived from Colombia and Mexico and flowed into the United States. He was easily the biggest-time dope dealer to come out of Venice, yet he didn't flaunt himself with gold and sports cars like some of the high rollers. He was known as the ten-million-dollar man. There were rumours that he was so rich now he was trying to get out of the business, but no one really knew. The guy was a mystery.

'Seems that the victim was Ricky Lee's mother,' said Cataresco.

'Yeah,' said Diamond. 'Musta put a dent in his day. Now he's under arrest for assaulting a police officer.'

Cataresco said that Richards had arrived on his own, not surrounded by his crew, and had asked if he could come in; when they'd said no, going by the book, he'd gone crazy, hitting one patrol guy in the stomach and butting another in the face before they could cuff him. 'That was when the crowd started showing up, and the press, boo-boo-*boo*.'

'Anyone from the DEA show up yet, or the Bureau?' There were so many good guys chasing drugs, all cranky about their acronyms and antsy for their budgets, all playing games with each other, all much too concerned with the size of their dicks, basically, that it was a miracle any big-time dealer ever got busted. The smart ones mostly didn't, and Ricky Lee was smart, but there were a lot of people trying to find out what was going on in his life. 'What about ATF, CRASH?'

'Not yet,' said Cataresco.

'Does he know she's dead?'

'I don't think so.'

Cataresco filled me in on what else they'd got. 'Victim's name Mae Richards, age forty-five, place of birth yeah yeah yeah you can read my report later. The body was found by a neighbour, one Louise Szell. She stopped by to ask if the victim would be going to church tonight. Evidently they usually walked together. She phoned in her report at three-thirty-one. No one heard a gunshot, no one heard or saw any signs of a struggle or anything untoward or unusual. Louise Szell said that someone did leave the house, about two-thirty, a guy, white, not young. Maybe fifty, fifty-five. He drove away in some fancy boat, a Cadillac or a Lincoln, dark colour, maybe grey or blue.'

'Plate?'

'She remembered three letters. GSG.'

Diamond chipped in, 'Gigli, Siepi, Gobbi.'

'Mafia guys?'

'Singers.'

Drew won that round. I turned to Cataresco, 'She reliable, this Louise . . .'

'Szell.'

'Right.'

'The neighbourhood busybody. Yeah, I'd say she's reliable.'

'That's something.' I went back to Diamond. 'There's a folded garbage bag in the sink.'

'I saw that,' he said. 'Maybe our shooter brought it with. Or somebody with our shooter.'

'Messages on the machine?'

'None, or wiped.'

Diamond had opened the fridge for a peek. 'I'm hungry,' he said to no one in particular. He picked a strawberry from the box on the counter. 'I hate strawberries,' he said. He ate one anyway.

This was the job, so much of it routine, an attempt to keep boredom at bay while assembling a picture of the past in terms of time and inches, like crawling on your hands and knees, trying to put back together a mosaic out of ancient pieces, tiny, millions of them, a near-infinity of details that must be re-created, and sometimes you never do find out which are the bits of gold, the ones that make the pattern.

Diamond and Cataresco would be there most of the rest of the night. They'd map the precise position of the corpse. They'd measure the dimensions of the kitchen and how far away from the body the spent cartridge had been found. They'd supervise the taking of prints and photos, and they'd go on gathering information about the victim. They'd watch while the coroner arrived and, to determine the time of death, slid a pointed thermometer into the victim's liver. It would make a popping noise, like bubble wrap.

Every murder cop goes about with a parasite in the heart. It's handy, this little worm. It eats up the feelings before they have time to reach the brain. In the end, though, there's the question: which will survive, the parasite or the man?

'I'd better go see Ricky Lee.'

'Go right ahead and be sympathetic,' said Diamond. 'But before you do, take a look at this.' He slipped on a pair of surgical gloves and, squatting by the side of the body, pushed his hand under and heaved it up gently. Mae Richards's hands were tied behind her back. The killer had sliced off the last joints, where the prints were. The ends of her fingers were stumps clogged with gore and bits of splintered bone.

Diamond said, 'Not too much blood. My guess is she was tortured and killed somewhere, then dumped back here.'

I wondered why the perpetrator had bothered to cut off her fingertips, usually done, along with smashing the teeth, to prevent an easy ID of the body – but pointless if the killer was going to leave the victim lying on her own kitchen floor. Perhaps she'd put up a fight after all, and the killer was on the ball enough to know the coroner would cut her fingernails to look for blood and skin tissue.

'What about the shell under the sink?'

'What about it?' said Diamond with a shrug.

'Any ideas?'

'Nope.'

'*Nope?*'

'Gee, Billy, don't start.'

'I'm sorry, excuse me, but I seem to see a dead body here. I don't know about you, Drew, but I'm out to *get* the murderers.'

He was about to say something, but I held up my hand. I said, 'Call me old-fashioned. Thieves I can live with. White-collar fraud, blue-collar rip-offs – be my guest. But let's think about rapists and child abusers. Let's think about *murderers*. It's unreasonable, of course, but it seems a good idea if maybe, *maybe*, guys like you and me step in and take a hand. What do you think, Drew?'

'Very funny, Billy,' he said, straightening his neck, squirming in his too-neat clothes.

'I'm not joking. Maybe the shell's not from the same weapon. Maybe it's a decoy. Maybe the perp was simple or wired or nuts. But someone really did this lady wrong, and I'm going to find him. Or her.'

On the way out I paused, attention caught by a framed photograph on top of a bookcase in the dining area, apart from the other family snaps. It showed Ricky Lee with one arm around the woman whose body was on the kitchen floor; in the other hand he held a tennis racquet. I slipped the photo out of its frame, into my pocket, and told Cataresco to remind Diamond about the garbage bag.

'He won't forget.'

'Remind him anyway.'

'Don't you think you should go a little easy on him?'

'Something about Drew makes me crazy. Maybe it's those fancy clothes he's started wearing. I don't know, but I'll tell you what – he's a loser.'

'Come on, Billy, the guy's been having a tough time. And you're riding him hard.'

'Fun, isn't it?'

I started to push my way through the crowd and past the reporters into the rain. The boy Nelson was there by my car, dripping and on his own. 'Hey, mister. Can I see your Beretta?' he said, as if asking for a quarter or candy.

Making a gun of my thumb and forefinger, I aimed it at him, and said, 'Pow!'

Jack Womack

Let's Put the Future Behind Us

'Toxic, merciless satire . . . I don't expect to read a funnier or more profound book this year.'   *Time Out*

'We can prove Kennedy shot himself – as long as we're paid in advance.'

In the unfettered freedom of Russia's new-found venture-capital frenzy, Max Borodin can organize anything – so long as the readies are ready. That's why he's Moscow's most successful businessman.

But Max's life has its downside: his wife, Tanya, nags him, his mistress, Sonya, exhausts him. Then there are always the country's friendly Mafia, keen to lend a helping hand with the profits of Max's Universal Manufacturing Company – producer of documents, historical and otherwise, to suit every conceivable occasion.

Satire rarely comes more sulphuric than this. *Let's Put the Future Behind Us* is the wittiest job of fictional surgery on New Russia since its iron curtain was amputated.

———————

Jack Womack is the author of the widely acclaimed *Random Acts of Senseless Violence*. His short fiction has appeared in *Omni* as well as various anthologies, and his journalism has appeared in *Spin*. He lives in New York.

Let's Put the Future Behind Us
Available now from Flamingo
ISBN 0 00 655007 X

ALLOW ME AN advertisement (an infomercial, I believe they are now called in America) for my central operation, founded four years ago. The Universal Manufacturing Company supplies a demanding public with needed documents. My trained specialists are accomplished at preparing notarized reports, business contracts, banking records, panegyrics issued by long-dead worthies, audits of production achievements worthy of material reward – in short, any paper that eases citizen life and warms bureaucratic hearts (excepting those aforementioned funerary officials, who are difficult). We can produce historic Soviet documents drawn to suit the demanding specifications of foreign journalists or officials. Prices are on a sliding scale; we would not charge a poor grandmother the same as the BBC or MTV. For now, the Universal Manufacturing Company deals strictly on a hard-currency basis. We use all modern overnight-express shipping services.

'Good morning, all,' I said, walking in. My well-paid staff joyfully responded, raising their heads from their desks, some for the moment pushing aside their lights and tools and engraving equipment. The long row of gentle *babushki* I keep busy preparing the small red folders in which internal passports are housed clucked and fluttered when I walked by them, as if they were hens and I a potent rooster. My senior workers smiled at my approach, and I gave them hearty greetings, stopping sometimes to inquire about a few long-term projects. 'How's it going?' I asked Fyodor, who worked on a project that held great interest for British researchers.

'Mr Philby has outwitted his superiors left and right,' Fyodor said, riffling a sheaf of superb-looking documents, 'but now he wishes to atone for his errors.'

I clapped him heartily on the back. Tomas, an excellent scribe who for many years worked in the competent organs in Nizhni Novgorod, raised his hand as I walked by, calling for my attention.

'Max?' he asked, showing me KGB documents to which he'd devoted unwavering attention for days. 'I need only appropriate signatures.'

'Pass it to Mischa, he can do them in his sleep,' I said, studying the paper; it was perfect. Tomas's assignment necessitated his producing a host of documents suggesting that CIA agents in Minsk foiled KGB attempts to brainwash Lee Harvey Oswald during the noted assassin's stay in our all-welcoming country. These documents were intended to eventually reach a well-known Chicago scholar, or so our middleman informed us. History can be so much more flexible than Lenin ever supposed; last May, Tomas supplied a California researcher with papers proving the precise opposite.

'The stamps are correct?' he asked.

'Reconfirm with Valentina.' In our contemporary world, past events are nothing more than zakuski, from which one selects delicious appetizers according to one's particular taste, and it pleases us to cater. The Universal Manufacturing Company can prove John Kennedy shot himself, as long as we are paid in advance.

When I stepped into my office suite my administrative assistant, Ludmilla, was already there. An aggressively responsible woman in her sixties, she believes deeply in her heart – as we all of us do here at Universal Manufacturing – that disturbing facts should never be too long hidden and thus relays unpleasant news every morning before I can even say hello.

'You have visitors and you'll not want to see them,' she told me.

'Who are they?'

'Evgeny, for one.'

My younger brother. 'Why is he here?'

'It would be beneath him to tell me, or so he seems to believe,' she said, making a sour face. 'Impress upon him that I am no public lackey. He's in your office.'

'He won't be for long. Who else?'

'Dmitry Mikhailovich Gubin.'

Sonya's husband. 'Where is he?'

'He went for a walk when I told him you hadn't yet arrived. Said he'll return at ten. He must talk to you, he insists. I told him he has no appointment and therefore it will depend on your discretion.'

'Did he say what he wanted?'

She shook her head. 'He appeared nervous.'

As any man might appear, coming to shoot his wife's lover. That, of course, was my initial unfounded reaction. For a moment I almost took my bulletproof vest out of the closet, but aging amateurs such as Dmitry rarely aim for the head, at least not on the first shot. I tried to throw off my gnawing fears. He could never have discovered our situation on his own, and Sonya would never confess. But what if he had? What if she did? At once my suspicions returned and began feeding on themselves. No emotion is so gaily self-cannibalistic as paranoia. I glanced behind me, in case he had crept back into the office, intent on revenge.

'Send him in when he returns,' I said, and stepped into my office. Evgeny sat in my comfortable chair, resting muddy shoes on my mahogany desk and perusing an issue of *The Economist*.

With brusque motions I shoved his feet back to the floor where they belonged.

'Max!' he exclaimed, quickly rising so that I might take the seat he so courteously warmed for me. 'A great opportunity presents itself.'

'Stop treating Ludmilla as if she were your lickspittle,' I said. 'We have no serfs here. Do you fancy yourself one of the false Romanovs?'

'She doesn't like me, Max. I have done nothing to her. She stares at me as if I were a spider, as if I'm evil personified.'

'Stupidity personified, perhaps. What do you want? It's too early to listen to your mad ideas.'

'Investors are interested in my park,' he said. 'It could mean big money for both of us. Is that too mad for you to hear?'

Evgeny is our family's holy fool. My brother will always be dear to me, but since childhood he has done all he can to test my love. For inexplicable reasons he perceives himself to be a master businessman, a financial whiz, my entrepreneurial equal. Evgeny could funnel money into a penned goose and never see a kopeck of it again. During the Brezhnev years, when even the little coma girl could have made millions of rubles while lying unconscious in her bed of trauma, Evgeny lost money in harebrained schemes. Under perestroika, when the lowest *zug* could get a handout from intelligent Westerners as long as an acceptable hatred of communism was feigned, Evgeny landed himself repeatedly into debt. Yet I must be fair and admit that he is not so much stupid as merely cursed with a soul innocent of guile. As a child he took too closely to heart our mother's fairy tales, and if today you were to tell him you had a magic hen for sale, he would open my wallet without a second's hesitation. 'Who is crazy enough?' I asked.

'Americans,' he said, almost hopping up and down with excitement. I must also admit that his most recent idea is not without merit. For two years he had devoted unstinting effort to developing a Western-style theme park to be located outside of Moscow. From a Polish consortium he borrowed money to purchase the land, and I had interest enough in the concept to sink seventy thousand dollars into preliminary construction. As of that morning, of course, only one building had been partially built.

'Were they on a tour bus?' I asked.

'They're from Texas,' he said, and then, in English, 'Howdy, partners.' Before hearing his call to the world of high finance, Evgeny wanted to be a cowboy. So often I wished that our parents had given him the horse he beseeched St Nicholas and the Snow Queen to bring him. 'They want to invest much money.'

'How did you meet them? What references do they have?' Proportionately, there are as many criminal Americans in Russia at present as there are criminal Russians, but not even the most respectable are here because of altruistic desires to assist our hard-beset people. Americans are our main competitors, uninterested in Russian prosperity and might unless it serves their purposes; only a fool denies it. Their business acumen is rarely as sharp as they think it to be, but Evgeny is perhaps the only Russian who could be constantly outwitted by Americans.

'Through your friend Gyorgi Ilyich,' he said, mentioning the name of a friend in the Ministry of Foreign Trade whose judgment I trusted. He had an unfortunate tendency to pass along information he thought useful to Evgeny without warning me beforehand. Granted, in the hands of anyone other than Evgeny the information could probably prove fruitful. 'I haven't met them. We spoke by phone. They stay at the Metropole and are utterly reliable, he says.'

'I want to meet them as well. I should assist in your presentation, I suppose?' My beloved brother nodded his head so rapidly I feared it would shake loose of his shoulders. I no longer allowed him to face wolves alone when they came seeking fresh lamb. 'When is a meeting scheduled?'

'In a few days.'

'You can't tell me?'

'I left my appointment book at my office.'

'All right,' I said, sighing. Always, I am encircled by fires onto which I must piss unending streams of money. Ludmilla appeared at the door.

'Mr Gubin has returned,' she said.

'Have him come in. Good-bye, Evgeny. Use the side exit.'

'Thank you again, Max.' As he bolted from the room, Dmitry Gubin entered. At a glance I saw he was unarmed and so at least felt assured of my physical security. To look at Dmitry, you would not have guessed he was incomparably more prosperous than he had been when he worked at the Ministry of Internal Affairs. He was flamboyantly nondescript. His old Hungarian suit was so stiff it might have been lined with cardboard, and his shoes had never come into proximity with leather. Dmitry's hair, what there was of it, was a greenish-gray blond. His hands, speckled with liver spots, showed nails bitten to the quick. It was lucky for him he had as much money as he did, for otherwise Sonya would not have looked twice at him except to laugh the louder.

'Come in, Dmitry Mikhailovich,' I said, although he had already sat down. There is no excuse to forget one's manners, however base the behaviour of those around you, but most of my countrymen will never learn this. 'How can I help?'

I braced myself to suffer, and thereafter deny, a torrent of accusations; but fate continued to be kind, and it soon became apparent to me that he had not come to discuss any unfortunate discoveries he might have made. 'I need to retain your specialists for an assignment, if you are willing to take me on as a client,' he said. 'Is your office secure, Maxim?'

'Absolutely,' I said. Every day two of my experts swept the office, protecting against electronic infiltration by malcontents, or spies wishing access to our trade secrets. 'Talk freely to me, as if you were in your own apartment.'

Judging from his expression, that was perhaps not so assuring a thought as I might have intended. 'Three friends and myself are setting up a new operation,' he began. 'They worked in the old Department for Combating Theft of Socialist Property.' I smiled. Dmitry may as well have confessed the crimes they'd not yet committed. The aforementioned department was corrupt even by Soviet standards; volunteers for such combat uniformly left the battlefield burdened by the fruits of victorious pillage while at arms. 'We will export souvenirs from Russia to Brighton Beach, New York, in exchange for hard currency.'

'Souvenirs?' I repeated. 'How many surplus medals and balalaikas does the world need?'

'A host of available markets remain,' Dmitry said, his mask as solemn as before. 'Our group is funding the operation, with some assistance by silent partners. We intend to work in partnership with another group responsible for oversight.'

'One of the more dependable mafias?' I asked, but he made no direct reply.

'Single representatives from our two groups are presently hammering out specifics of our partnership. These negotiations will conclude by the end of February. What I need done needs to be done before then.'

'Broader investigations will be undertaken at the conclusion of negotiations?' Such was standard procedure; one can be no less careful in choosing partners for business than for marriage – should be more careful, in most cases.

'Exactly,' he said. 'The representatives will exchange complete membership information and afterwards will make background checks of all participants. Once the reliability of those involved is assured, the contract will be signed, we'll meet for formal celebrations, the programme goes forth. Standard procedure.'

There was of course a great deal Dmitry was not telling me, but that was as it should be. 'I congratulate you on your initiative, but you've not come to boast of your marketing prowess. What do you want us to do?' I paused long enough to give him a most necessary caveat. 'Don't relate information which doesn't directly bear upon the proposed assignment.'

By making that statement and preserving it on tape, I could later defend myself against charges of conspiracy, if charges were for any reason ever filed – my lawyer assured me that it is a foolproof procedure. (I have a new lawyer, now.) Dmitry stared at me for an interminable time before speaking. Again, I felt a disconcerting chill along my spine; this was prelude, I thought anew, a distraction before his attack began – but I was wrong. Leaning forward, whispering, he said, 'I will have to give you *some* background. You remember the railroad scandal?'

'Of course.' The railroad scandal was, I think, the most breathtaking swindle perpetrated during the Brezhnev regime; granted, the competition is fierce. A railroad through Georgia was proposed and designed. The go-ahead was given. Every kopeck of the millions of rubles allocated for the project was siphoned off during the four-year period of so-called construction. In most of the world, secrets known to more than one are no longer secrets; but in our incomparable land, millions know secrets and they remain secrets. The multitude eventually involved in the scheme not only conspired to pretend that the railroad was being built, continuing after its theoretical completion to claim that the railroad truly existed, but went one step – a staircase! – beyond by providing and forwarding to the unsuspecting agencies solid proof that the imaginary railroad was one of the most productive in the Soviet Union. I have read much in western magazines recently concerning the supposed new field of virtual reality; has there ever been any other kind in Russia? 'You were involved?'

'Very much so,' he said, his eyes wary as a cornered rabbit's.

Jack Womack

'This casts a shadow over present situations?'

'Very much so,' he repeated, sighing as if guilt caused him physical pain. 'When deputy ministers are themselves involved, is it so shocking that those under them would also be? I was no mastermind, no Napoleon of crime, but if advantage could be taken, you took it.' Unexpectedly his face lost its lines of care, and I could not imagine what elation seized his heart until I realized he was under the impression he was confessing to one who in spirit, if not in act, was but another stalwart in corruption. 'You remember those years, Max. The most of the most.'

'I am not threatening you with the gulag, Dmitry. What is your point?'

From his brow he wiped fear's morning dew. 'I am telling you I was but one of many semi-innocents, that is all. Unlike most of the idiots involved, some of us saved our money so that when Andropov's dogs came sniffing, we could buy needed influence. But money wasn't enough, sometimes. It's been all I could do to live with my conscience, since.'

'Lived well, I'd say.'

He ignored my remark. 'Pressure was put upon us by the competent organs. We were given an opportunity to redeem ourselves by serving our nation patriotically through the sharing of information. I did what I could, several of us did. We passed along potentially useful facts regarding a key cadre of plotters in Tbilisi, of whose existence the authorities were unaware. Its members were prosecuted and convicted and shipped to Archangel, excepting the one who was executed. My God, Max, you wouldn't expect Georgians to thrive in such cold country.' He shuddered as if he too had for too long been flash-frozen.

'They survived and have returned?' I asked.

'Understand that my present associates, who were innocent of involvement in the railroad scandal, were the ones who initiated our current deal. Once it was under way, what could I do?'

'You're telling me the group with whom you'll be in partnership includes the same Georgians you helped send to prison?'

'Some of them.'

'Are they aware of your guilt?' I asked. 'If not, they'll ascertain your complicity when they look into the records.'

'Precisely my point,' he said. 'They don't know me yet; I would have been nothing to them at the time. It was only a happy accident that I knew of their involvement. Not so happy, now. I was told the reports I made were entered anonymously, but who knows for sure? When the Georgians make their search, they may find suggestive material. It would be only human for them to leap to conclusions.'

'Why don't you make new deals, with safer partners?' I asked. 'That's my recommendation.'

'This deal is unmatchable, Maxim,' he said. 'An astonishing opportunity.'

'To peddle souvenirs like a pensioner in street markets?'

'*Blyad!*' he shouted, and hot words erupted like lava from his mouth. 'There's money enough in this deal to enable Sonya and me to leave this insane country!'

'That's your intention?' I asked, knowing I revealed no disconcertion in my features. Sonya had told me nothing of any plans to emigrate.

'What kind of life are we living here, Max? We are prosperous, sure. We command respect. We enjoy business success, we own fine apartments, we possess priceless treasures. We live like kings, but we live in a pigsty. Here shit, there shit. What kind of life is that for human beings?'

'These are Russia's most difficult hours, Dmitry, but —'

'But what? Wait till the future? How long have we heard such lies about our radiant future? Look out your window, tell me what our future will be.'

'What I was going to tell you is we should make what we can of the present,' I said. 'Let's put the future behind us.'

'I am trying to make everything I can of the present,' he told me. 'You say not to tell you more than is necessary. Very well, it is necessary that I be in on this deal, whatever the dangers. It is necessary that the records are corrected. The world waits for me, and I want to go there.' Dmitry halted his tirade and paused, gasping for breath. 'Can you do the job?'

'Of course, but it is complex,' I said. 'Several thousand documents will be involved in such a case as you describe. They must be found, destroyed, replaced. Plus checks in KGB records. Maybe in SVRR, or even the GRU. All this to be done in a month and a half. And I don't have to tell you, the bureaucrats with whom we deal will have to be greased until they're slippery as eels.'

'That doesn't fuck me,' he said. 'No one but you can even grasp the enormity of the problem, much less solve it.'

'The problem itself is not my sole concern. Georgians are dangerous. The idea of working with them even at a distance troubles me.'

'Certainly I sympathize with your fear,' Dmitry said.

'Then you understand why I cannot –'

'One million dollars, American. Three hundred now, the remainder once our deal is concluded. Would this sum bolster your courage?'

Though usually I am as adept as Tanya at cloaking honest emotions beneath a facade of cool impassiveness, I feel sure Dmitry discerned the shock I felt, hearing him name his sum. 'Why do you need money to move if you can provide such a fee for our services?'

'For our project my group, not I, have funding sufficient for our needs. What do you say, Max?'

The pashas and beys of the Sultan were yet waiting to be greeted. But who could predict how they might respond to my enticements? One million dollars, and I could hear every bill rustling like leaves in the wind. 'Give me until tomorrow to decide.'

'He has whispered these dreams in my ears before. Why should I believe him?' Sonya asked me that evening, in the tiny apartment off Arbat Street I rent specifically to assure undisturbed privacy for our evening trysts. 'My darling, it's too ridiculous to warrant consideration. He and I are not leaving Russia, don't worry. You and I are capable people, sure, but what would Dmitry do, anywhere else?'

'He has his talents,' I noted, but I remained unconvinced that I could enumerate them, if called upon to do so. She stroked my arms with feather's touch and rubbed her legs against mine as if to set them ablaze. There aren't words enough for me to say how dearly I love my wife, for all our trials, but I would be lying if I didn't tell you that when I was with Sonya I wished to be nowhere else. Already once that evening we had made mad love, and now she bided her time while I regained my strength.

'Just to smuggle his priceless treasures out of Russia would cost him the money he is already busy counting,' she said. 'Dmitry is so smart, he is stupid. And these partners of his are no wiser, I assure you.'

'He's told you nothing about this project?' I asked again. 'Not even a hint?'

She shook her head. I felt unspeakable delight, marvelling at my goddess's gold hair gleaming in the room's winter moonlight. 'Why should it matter that you know what they're up to? Isn't it written in your contracts that you should know nothing about nothing?'

'This is different,' I said. 'Too many uncertainties. There's this involvement with Georgians. His cagey references to silent partners. And so much money. There is something dark under way, I think.'

'If Dmitry wants to give you this mountain of money, take it,' she said. 'I would prefer that you were the one so burdened with wealth.'

'If he's involved in malfeasance you're involved as well, my angel.' Embracing me, she raked her fingernails along my sides. The stimulating pain she inflicted with her talons made me more aware of my apprehension. 'You may be burned if he's juggling fire.' It was difficult to speak with an extra tongue in my mouth; I pulled away from her. 'This project may keep him in such proximity to me that it may be harder for us to see each other. Have you thought of that?' Striking with astonishing speed, she hit her target with unerring accuracy, once more fastening her lips onto mine. We kissed as if to inhale each other's souls. 'Look, if his plan succeeds, and he's serious, he'll leave and take you with him. And I'll have helped him take you from me.'

'Why should I leave unless I want to?' she asked, bringing her face so close to mine that I thought I glimpsed ball lightning leaping between our eyes. 'I'll go nowhere I don't want to go. He can juggle whatever he wants.'

'It could be dangerous.'

Sonya stopped my mouth with a nipple, quieting her infant. As she bade me suck she pushed my head and shoulders against our bed's headboard. A small *matryoshka* doll tumbled onto the mattress. 'There is danger walking down any street,' she said. 'Danger here with you too, I think.'

As she took my ear in her mouth she carefully replaced her doll on the headboard, which was lined with our room's *poshlaia*, an army of *matryoshkas*. *Matryoshkas* are Russia's own Barbies, small wooden dolls that hold, nestling within them, a series of progressively smaller wooden dolls: open the first and find another, and then another. Traditionally, each doll is a replica of the one that encases it, but in recent years the artists are perhaps reacting as artists often subconsciously do to transformations in their societies, as the peasant smells the storm in the wind. When you open a *matryoshka* of contemporary vintage, there is no foretelling what pleasant or unpleasant discoveries may be found within.

'Mutual danger,' I said.

Sonya revealed her teeth and then turned away, crawling serpentlike to the foot of our bed. She curled over the edge, placing her hands on the floor. My eyes were drawn to the end of Sonya that conveys the purest and most essential expression. She wriggled her backside, as if her unseen front half were helplessly caught. My response to that particular action of hers was Pavlovian: my well-worn implement rose up to beg unconditionally for its honeyed treat. 'Decadent Western music should accompany our sins, don't you think?' she said, switching on her tape player. I grimaced as she added her own atonal purr to those deafening American yodels. Backing up, lifting her hips, she spread her long legs so I could better focus on the apex of her pyramid.

'Come pin your butterfly.'

'*Koshka!*' I exclaimed. Making a great leap forward, I buried my face in her underbeard, and as I lapped up her sweet nectar, tasting of mushrooms and honey, her feral moans counterpointed those of her favoured artists. Rolling onto her back, she seized my neck with her hands as if to break it, arched her spine, and clamped her legs around me, pinching my sides in an iron grip. During our maniacal storm of passion she gasped, shrieked, wept, and gnashed her teeth. She flailed her arms so wildly she left bruises where she struck me, but I barely noticed and couldn't have cared less (I would take pains later to be sure Tanya did not see them). It was hot work in the sweatshop. The Bolshevik Alexandra Kollontai (whom romantic if wrongheaded revisionists have recently called Lenin's mistress) is notorious for having said that in our unprecedented revolutionary society sexual intercourse should be no less necessary, or more remarkable, than the act of drinking a glass of water. I could not imagine that Sonya's thirst would ever be slaked.

Afterward we lay on damp sheets, clasped tightly, as if we could burrow beneath each other's skin. Her music, mercifully, came to an end. We listened instead to the argument of the couple who lived next door and to trucks grinding gears as their drivers sped down the lanes of the nearby Garden Ring.

'Tell him you'll do it.' Her voice was a moist whisper.

One million dollars. 'I don't know.'

'Tell him. Believe me, I won't go with him if he emigrates. And if there's danger in what he does, who better to protect me from danger than you?'

Hundreds, perhaps thousands would be better equipped; that is, after all, what security forces are for. 'He'll be constantly lurking around. Even the blindest hog finds truffles.'

'Dmitry could be in the next room now and never know we were in here together, naked. He is too preoccupied with his grand schemes. With his treasures. Tell me, how could he ever know of our love?'

'If you tell him.'

Sonya ran angel's fingers along the length of me. 'One raven never pecks out the eyes of another.'

'I'll speak to him tomorrow,' I said, as she started to lick my neck. Gunshots, outside, sounded as celebratory fireworks. What a joyous city is Moscow.

cult fiction

flamingo

supported by

W

WATERSTONE'S

www.waterstones.co.uk

THE TIMES
www.4-D.co.uk

Infectious Records
www.infectiousxxx.co.uk

Book Rock and The Paradise Motel

The Paradise Motel – REWORKINGS

Following the release of their acclaimed album FLIGHT PATHS, The Paradise Motel have called upon the talents of a number of bands and artists they admire to rework some of their songs. The results are to be released September '99 on a double CD alongside the original versions.

The Trees – reworked by Lee Ranaldo of Sonic Youth
Drive – the Cars classic reworked by Mogwai
Cities – reworked by Mark Eitzel, latterly of American Music Club
BH Rock – as reworked by Bows (*aka* Luke Sutherland)
Derwent River Star – reworked by Echoboy
Four Degrees – reworked by Too Pure recording artists Hefner
Hollywood Landmines – the recent single reworked by Blue Mar Ten
(infect65cdx)

To coincide with the release of REWORKINGS, The Paradise Motel will be playing special acoustic shows in a number of bookshops in the UK Autumn / Winter '99. Check local listings for details.

Also available: LEFT OVER LIFE TO KILL (infect47cd) – the debut album.

'They break the heart again and again . . . ★★★★' **Q magazine**

'Dreamlike and deadly' **Uncut**

All releases available on Infectious Records, distributed via Vital.

www.infectiousxxx.co.uk

contact: feedback@infectious.co.uk or the band direct:
keepsafe@hotmail.com

Henry Miller

Tropic of Cancer

With an introduction by Robert Nye

A penniless and as yet unpublished writer, Henry Miller arrived in Paris in 1930. Leaving behind a disintegrating marriage and an unhappy career in America, he threw himself into the low-life of Bohemian Paris with unwavering gusto. A fictional account of Miller's adventures amongst the prostitutes and pimps, the penniless painters and writers of Montparnasse, *Tropic of Cancer* is an extravagant and rhapsodic hymn to a world of unrivalled eroticism and freedom.

'A rhapsody deriving from Whitman, Joyce, Lawrence and Céline, *Tropic of Cancer* is a ranting, randy book carried along by a deep, sensual enjoyment of living.' *Sunday Times*

'*Tropic of Cancer* is a great prophetic book, a warning of what deadens life, an affirmation that it can yet be lived, though with extreme difficulty, in an age whose sterile non-cultures seek to thwart all mainsprings of fertility. Miller reveals himself as a battered faun, a crafty innocent, a lonely, lazy, sometimes fearful, always steadfast, worshipper of life.' Colin MacInnes, *Spectator*

flamingo

Jim Lewis

Why the Tree Loves the Axe

'A clever, weird, utterly absorbing story told by a rare talent.'
The Times

'Caroline is a compulsive liar. She ends up in Sugartown, Texas, after fleeing a broken marriage and suffering a car crash, and makes up an identity for herself to get a job. She lives a shadowy fictionalised life as an orderly in a geriatric ward, getting involved with a sinister old man, who confers on her a strange box to deliver, and a soul-mate girlfriend whom she strangely resembles. Sugartown descends into hellish street riots during which Caroline kills a policeman, and learns that her girlfriend has died . . .

'Jim Lewis deserves a wider audience . . . The narrative here is modern American Gothic, with a Pinteresque menace, and a nice twist in the tale . . . Lewis covers a wonderful range of American experiences. Midwest pieties and dreams of a new city on the plain are transformed into a nightmare of social unrest, sinister geriatric decay and necessary lawlessness . . . wise, lyrical and refreshingly astonishing.'
ADAM PIETTE, *Evening Standard*

'A literary suspense novel that actually delivers – a page turner that will keep readers guessing until the end, their curiosity fuelled as much by the book's gorgeously inventive imagery as by its seductive plot.'
SARAH FERGUSON, *New York Times*

'By releasing the tallest of stories in a rush of rich language, Jim Lewis dazzles you into credulity. An unmissable novel.'
She

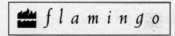 flamingo

Jack Kerouac

Dharma Bums

'Kerouac's energy is contagious, his compassion and concern
are the genuine homespun article.' *Guardian*

Ray Smith is a coast-to-coast, freight-hopping poet and
drifter, at odds with urban life and middle-class existence
('all that dumb white machinery in the kitchen'). He meets a
kindred spirit in Japhy Rider, a Buddhist drop-out, who
enlists Ray into a regime of crazy, purifying hikes up the
peaks of the High Sierra and non-stop Zen Free Love Lunacy
orgies. 'Two dissimilar monks on the one path', their haphaz-
ard, often hilarious search for the contentment of 'dharma',
Buddhism's all pervading, supreme principle of life, is pure
Kerouac.

The Dharma Bums' cry for a 'great rucksack revolution' in
which the country's youth would cast off the everyday, take
to the open road and live the Buddhist way, inspired a whole
generation of post-war Americans to search for spiritual
knowledge and self-transcendence.

'The Beat Generation now looks quaint to today's loose freaks
who take for granted stances that the rebels of the Fifties only
strained toward. But if the Beat lifestyle and attitudes were
essentially crude experiments leading to the cultural revolution of the Sixties, it's still certain that what sparse literature
the counter-culture has produced sings nowhere as vibrant,
strong and original as in Kerouac.' *Rolling Stone*

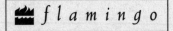 *flamingo*

Richard Beard

Damascus

'It's the last day of the holidays and Spencer Kelly (12) wants
to hold Hazel Burns (12) by the hand. This is the meaning of
life. He wants to sit beside her on a sand dune and hold her
hand and then kiss her. Just kissing, in a nice way, on her
cheek perhaps and then a little bit at the top of her arms . . . If
he can kiss her this once then he'll always have kissed her,
and everything which follows will be different. It's to be the
one moment which instantly changes everything.'

'Richard Beard's second novel is something of an event, given
the widespread plaudits for his first. In that book, *X 20*, he
arranged an ingenious and unconventional structure around
tobacco smoking. In his new novel Beard uses similar tech-
niques, but this time in a romance . . . Beard is a talented
writer, crafting many scenes with luminous precision.'

PETER CARTY, *Time Out*

'The climactic showdown is not only an apt marriage of the
novel's form and content . . . but also gently comic, the charac-
teristic tone of this undertaking. Ludic in a peculiarly British
manner . . . an assured achievement.'

STEPHEN KNIGHT, *TLS*

'Lovely, funny, touching, and exciting.'

HARRY MATHEWS, author of *The Journalist*

'A book with a real difference.'   *Irish News*

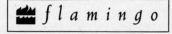

Aldous Huxley

The Doors of Perception
Heaven and Hell

With a Foreword by J. G. Ballard

'Concise, evocative, wise and, above all, humane, *The Doors of Perception* is a masterpiece.' *Sunday Times*

One bright May morning in 1953, Aldous Huxley took four-tenths of a gramme of mescalin, sat down and waited to see what would happen. When he opened his eyes, everything, from the flowers in a vase to the creases in his grey flannel trousers, was completely transformed. 'A bunch of flowers shining with their own inner light. Those folds – what a labyrinth of endlessly significant complexity! I was seeing what Adam had seen on the morning of his own creation – the miracle, moment by moment, of naked existence.'

With an astonishing immediacy, Aldous Huxley described his first experience of this new 'sacramental vision of reality' in his famous 1954 essay *The Doors of Perception*. In its 1956 sequel, *Heaven and Hell*, Huxley, reflecting on his earlier mescalin experience, went on to explore the history and nature of mystics and mysticism. Hugely influential, still bristling with a sense of excitement and discovery, these intense and illuminating writings remain the most extraordinary accounts of the visionary experience ever written.

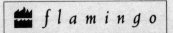 *flamingo*

Ben Marcus

The Age of Wire and String

'Genuinely original'   *The Times*

'Transfixing . . . an extraordinary debut . . . Most contemporary
fiction is afraid to make the reader work hard for understanding, and in consequence the reader's rewards are smaller. But
The Age of Wire and String, a treasury of interconnected fables
of violence and hope, stands out as an exhilarating work of
literature. Multiple readings are rewarding.'

STEVEN POOLE, *TLS*

'*The Age of Wire and String* evades classification, persisting in
your mind because of its psychotically ardent prose. It
contains no debased images, no second-hand symbols. It will
find its fans among those people who relish prose that mimics
dream, who love it when words are used as they once were,
as incantations, as spells to summon up the contorted beings
of the imagination.'   MATTHEW DE ABAITUA, *The Idler*

'Frequently touching and funny, plenty of madness, magic
and gods . . . a cross between a scientific manual, *Monty
Python* and a kind of Bible, with a surreal and opaque logic of
its own.'   CHRISTINA PATTERSON, *Observer*

flamingo

Tim O'Brien
Going After Cacciato

One rainy day in Vietnam a pleasant, moon-faced soldier named Cacciato decides that, all things considered, he'd rather be in Paris, even if he has to walk there, all 8,600 miles. The men of Third Squad, First Platoon, Alpha Company, set out in pursuit – to find him, to bring him back. The result is a magnificent journey of the imagination through war and peace. Part dream, part reality, this extraordinary and beautiful novel has been hailed as a modern classic.

Winner of
THE 1979 NATIONAL BOOK AWARD FOR FICTION

'*Going After Cacciato* is not only a brilliant and moving novel about the war in Vietnam, it is about all wars and their profound physical, emotional and moral effect upon the men who serve in them. His irony recalls that of Stendhal, his landscapes have the breadth and scope of Tolstoy's and the essential American wonder and innocence of his vision deserves to stand beside that of Stephen Crane.' National Book Award Citation

'Powerful and haunting . . . the best novel to have come out of Vietnam.' *Sunday Telegraph*

'A major achievement . . . to call *Going After Cacciato* a novel about war is like calling *Moby Dick* a novel about whales. Clearly we are dealing here with "magical realism". Tim O'Brien's writing is crisp, authentic and grimly ironic.'
  New York Times Book Review

'Not only the best novel about the Vietnam War, but among the finest works of fiction in contemporary American literature.'
  PHILIP CAPUTO, *Esquire*

ISBN 0 00 654307 3

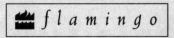 flamingo

Hubert Selby Jr

Last Exit to Brooklyn

With an introduction by Anthony Burgess

Last Exit to Brooklyn is a raw depiction of life amongst New York's junkies, hustlers, drag queens and prostitutes. An unforgettable cast of characters inhabits the housing projects, bars and streets of Brooklyn: Georgette, a hopelessly romantic and tormented transvestite; Vinnie, a disaffected and volatile youth who has never been on the right side of the law; Tralala, who can find no escape from her loveless existence; Harry, a power-hungry strike leader with a fatal secret. Living on the edge, always walking on the wild side, their alienation and aggression masks a desperate, deep need for affection and kinship.

Banned in Britain on first publication in 1964, *Last Exit to Brooklyn* brought its ex-marine, drug-addict author instant notoriety. Its truthfulness stunned a generation and continues to shock to this day.

'It is the clash of aspiration, fantasy and desire with the boundaries of the purely contingent that provides the drama of Selby's work and its ferocious poetry.'   *TLS*

'Selby's place is in the front rank of American novelists . . . so to understand his work is to understand the anguish of America.'   *New York Times*

ISBN 0 586 08588 2

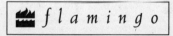

£1 off

flamingo

W

WATERSTONE'S

This voucher entitles you to £1.00 off *Microserfs*, and is redeemable only at Waterstone's. This voucher is not transferable and is only redeemable against *Microserfs*.
The closing date for this offer is 30/4/2000.

TO THE RETAILER: This voucher will be redeemed ONLY if it has been taken in part payment for the purchase of *Microserfs* featured in this sampler. HarperCollins*Publishers* reserve the right to refuse payment against misredeemed vouchers. Please submit vouchers by 31/06/2000, to Avril Cowan, Customer Services, HarperCollins*Publishers*, Glasgow, G4 0BR

£1 off

flamingo

W

WATERSTONE'S

This voucher entitles you to £1.00 off *Bordersnakes*, and is redeemable only at Waterstone's. This voucher is not transferable and is only redeemable against *Bordersnakes*.
The closing date for this offer is 30/4/2000.

TO THE RETAILER: This voucher will be redeemed ONLY if it has been taken in part payment for the purchase of *Bordersnakes* featured in this sampler. HarperCollins*Publishers* reserve the right to refuse payment against misredeemed vouchers. Please submit vouchers by 31/06/2000, to Avril Cowan, Customer Services, HarperCollins*Publishers*, Glasgow, G4 0BR

£1 off

W

WATERSTONE'S

Harper
Collins

This voucher entitles you to £1.00 off *Florida Roadkill*, and is redeemable only at Waterstone's. This voucher is not transferable and is only redeemable against *Florida Roadkill*.
The closing date for this offer is 30/4/2000.

TO THE RETAILER: This voucher will be redeemed ONLY if it has been taken in part payment for the purchase of *Florida Roadkill* featured in this sampler. HarperCollins*Publishers* reserve the right to refuse payment against misredeemed vouchers. Please submit vouchers by 31/06/2000, to Avril Cowan, Customer Services, HarperCollins*Publishers*, Glasgow, G4 0BR

£1 off

flamingo

W

WATERSTONE'S

This voucher entitles you to £1.00 off *The Restraint of Beasts*, and is redeemable only at Waterstone's. This voucher is not transferable and is only redeemable against *The Restraint of Beasts*.
The closing date for this offer is 30/4/2000.

TO THE RETAILER: This voucher will be redeemed ONLY if it has been taken in part payment for the purchase of *The Restraint of Beasts* featured in this sampler. HarperCollins*Publishers* reserve the right to refuse payment against misredeemed vouchers. Please submit vouchers by 31/06/2000, to Avril Cowan, Customer Services, HarperCollins*Publishers*, Glasgow, G4 0BR

cult fiction

Cult Fiction is a free sampler containing extracts from
ten full-length works of fiction.

The ten vouchers below entitle you to £1.00 off the price of
the books featured in this sampler when you purchase them –
at branches of Waterstone's only.

WATERSTONE'S

WATERSTONE'S

This voucher entitles you to £1.00 off *Cocaine Nights*, and is redeemable only at Waterstone's. This voucher is not transferable and is only redeemable against *Cocaine Nights*.
The closing date for this offer is 30/4/2000.

TO THE RETAILER: This voucher will be redeemed ONLY if it has been taken in part payment for the purchase of *Cocaine Nights* featured in this sampler. HarperCollins*Publishers* reserve the right to refuse payment against misredeemed vouchers. Please submit vouchers by 31/06/2000, to Avril Cowan, Customer Services, HarperCollins*Publishers*, Glasgow, G4 0BR

WATERSTONE'S

This voucher entitles you to £1.00 off *Naked Lunch*, and is redeemable only at Waterstone's. This voucher is not transferable and is only redeemable against *Naked Lunch*.
The closing date for this offer is 30/4/2000.

TO THE RETAILER: This voucher will be redeemed ONLY if it has been taken in part payment for the purchase of *Naked Lunch* featured in this sampler. HarperCollins*Publishers* reserve the right to refuse payment against misredeemed vouchers. Please submit vouchers by 31/06/2000, to Avril Cowan, Customer Services, HarperCollins*Publishers*, Glasgow, G4 0BR